Dynastii & Tec

Shawty Fell for a Boss

Trenae'

Trenae Presents

This book is dedicated to my heart and my headache, Ava Marie. There's no limit to what I would do to make sure there is always a smile on your face, gorgeous. Nanny loves you to the moon and back.

To my sister, Asia Lewis. We the girls of the crew and swear we stay live! I can't thank you enough for giving me the opportunity to know and love Ava! Love ya gah.

To my brother, Kevin Lewis Jr. My giant I'm so proud of you for following your dreams and never giving up. You went to college and dominated the court as well as those classes and graduation is coming up. Love you my big lil brother.

Contents

Acknowledgments:

Ninth book Shawttttyyy!!!! Lol

This part never gets easy because of course I don't want to miss anyone. First and foremost, I want to thank God for giving me the gift of storytelling. I'm still shocked that I can actually create a story that you, my readers, love. It baffles me that I went through so much schooling just to end up coming back to what I've always loved, writing. I know that that was no one but God's doing. Without him there would be no Trenae' and for that I am forever grateful.

To my fiance' and best friend, Joe. You are the most supportive boyfriend a girl could ask for. You accept when I can't pay attention to you because I'm chasing the bag, you motivate me when I feel like giving up, you allow me to bounce ideas off of you and you even throw out titles. (Even if they suck and I never use them lol). I love you because even when I'm a mess, you love me. When I'm working on a book, I know I look a mess on the regular, but you still tell me I'm the prettiest girl ever. I'm grateful for the times you start meals and clean the kitchen so that I can work. You are an amazing man and an amazing father. I love you forever and a day!

To my parents, Trudy, Keith and Tarunye thank you for the continued support. As soon as I say my book is live y'all quickly one-click and I definitely appreciate it.

To the women who played a huge role in raising me, my grandmother Deloris, my aunt Betty and my aunt Mona, I appreciate every sacrifice you made to make sure I never went without anything I needed. Thank you for all that y'all do.

To my siblings, Kevin, Malika, Asia, Tarya, Makia, and Jayanma I love y'all and never forget that the sky is the limit.

1

To my Godchild and constant headache, Ava, anything that I do is for you! It's my job to make sure that smile never falls from your face and I'll work overtime to make sure that happens. Nanny loves you forever and a day Phat-Phat!

To my cousins that are more like siblings, Raquel, Reggie, Trevor and Boots I love y'all!

To my squuuuuaaaadddd lol, Chrissy, Fantasia and Kelleashia bruh so many of y'all stories find their way into my books. My characters are based off of y'all and everything, thanks for the constant laughs. Above all that thanks for remaining the same, y'all never switched up on the kid and I appreciate that. You know y'all stuck with me foreva (Cardi B voice).

Keondria, Secret, Kelleashia, and Rikida, I can't thank y'all enough for the brutal honesty y'all give me. Y'all been rocking with me since The Sins of Beretta one and as I end their story here you are all, still by my side. Y'all the best.

To my sisters of KBC thanks for y'all continued support, Love y'all.

Last but most certainly not least, to YOU my readers, I cannot thank you all enough for continuing to rock with me. Y'all took a chance on a new author and I will strive to never let y'all down. Thanks for the inboxes and reviews on my past work, I definitely took everything y'all said into consideration. I have to also thank y'all for being patient with me, as I got this book done for you all.

If I missed anyone know that it wasn't intentional. Charge my memory and not my heart for that mistake.

I hope you enjoy my this read because these characters took me for a ride and never stopped talking to me!

Want to keep up with Trenae'?
Facebook: Paree Trenae
Facebook: Author Trenae'

Instagram: Trenaedhaplug

Twitter: Ooh_Paree_Dear

Snapchat: PareeTrenae

Periscope: PareeTrenae

Add my reader's group: Trenae' Presents: The Juice

Synopsis:

****THIS WAS ORIGINALLY AN INCOMPLETE SERIES (FIRST LADY OF THE STREETS) THAT IS NOW BEING **RERELEASED** AS A COMPLETE STANDALONE****

If you go through hell and make it back, then you have nothing to fear. Dynastii is a walking testament of this phrase. After life gave her hell in the form of kidnapping the love of her life; her son, she has no choice other than turning to the streets. Ignoring the warnings from her boyfriend of six years President "Prez" Pierre; Dynastii is a scorned mother causing havoc until she gets some answers.

Dynastii knew to expect drugs, money, & murder when she jumped back into the game. The only thing she didn't expect was the laid-back boss she meets named Tec. Without hesitation Tec came in & showed her everything she deserved and wasn't getting with Prez. Dynastii soon finds herself torn between being loyal to Prez and finding new love with Tec. Her decision is easily made when Prez does the unthinkable basically giving her the green light to fall for a boss.

Like most men, Tec has a pass that. The difference is, his past isn't ready to allow him to see a future without her in it. Ashanti loves no one but herself and her money. With Tec being her walking ATM machine, she isn't ready to let a new woman come in and cause her well to run dry. Her greed knows no limits and when it causes her secrets to become exposed, she has nothing left to do but turn to the very friend she wronged.

With skeletons dancing around in everyone's closet two question remains. Will Dynastii get the answers to her son's murder and will she allow herself to fall for a boss with a past?

The Beginning to the end

Dynastii

"Damn Dy, that's how the fuck you wake a nigga up," Prez moaned with his eyes rolling to the back of his head as his dick disappeared down my throat. Opening wide, I allowed him to fuck my mouth until his seeds were pouring down my throat.

"Good morning baby, get yourself together and I'll have breakfast on the table." I smiled jumping up and heading to the bathroom.

Brushing my teeth, I admired the huge rock on my finger. Despite how long Prez and I had been dating this wasn't an engagement ring. His grown ass presented me with a promise ring when we hit our sixth-year anniversary. His promise was when he hit whatever outrageous amount of money that he felt was enough to walk away from the game he would marry me. I knew that was bullshit, but what do you do when you love a man as much as I loved President Pierre. You wear the fuck out of that promise ring and dare a bitch to snicker about it.

"Good looking out ma, what are you cooking this morning?" Prez walked in kissing me on the forehead.

"I was thinking pancakes, eggs, sausage, and grits, is that cool?"

"Yeah, I'm hungry as fuck so make sure you fix me a big plate." I nodded and walked out of the room before the print in his boxers made me start some shit. Prez was fine and he knew it, standing at 6'1 and 220 pounds of muscle how could he not know it? I wasn't normally into bright guys but from the moment I met him he just did something to me. At a young age, he had me doing shit no teenager had business doing. I'm the type of bitch that if my man said he wanted to be an ice cream man I was in the back scooping, and if he wanted to be a basketball coach then I was in the gym shooting. So, it's only natural that when his right-hand man got knocked I was in the traps serving fiends, breaking down weed, bagging dope, counting out any type of pills you could name, and measuring syrup. I wasn't new to any of that shit; behind my nigga, I had even caught a few bodies all with the taste of Similac still on my breath. Before getting pregnant with our son, Malakhi, it was normal to see me in the hood causing havoc but for my baby boy I became the type of woman he would be proud of. I left the hood alone and enrolled into school. Within weeks I had my G.E.D and I was now going to school for business.

I paused outside of Malakhi's room and listened to see if he was up. He was so active that at seventeen months he would be catching flips in his crib. I loved him, but I refused to open the door to peep in because his ass would pop up from a deep sleep. Walking down the stairs, I thanked God for my blessings. I went from homeless to the projects and now my family and I called the six-bedroom four-bathroom home ours. Material things weren't everything, but I'll be damned if I wasn't happier living here than I was sleeping in the projects. After turning on Spotify and going to my Anita Baker playlist, it wasn't long before the dining room table was filled with food.

"Damn ma, you hooked it up!" I jumped from Prez's voice.

"Didn't I tell yo ass about creeping up on me. Make some noise nigga, announce yourself when stepping in a room," I said, placing the gun back in the kitchen cabinet. I don't know how he did it but Prez could walk in any room and you wouldn't know he was there, and his ass could hear an ant pissing in the neighbor's yard.

"Yo ass stays walking around with guns, but swears you aren't street material anymore. I told you just because you were a mama didn't mean you had to become boring," he said, kissing his teeth.

"I'm not street material because I'm mommy material, nigga. I can't be both! The hood won't ever leave me, but I did leave the hood to give my child more than I had. Most niggas want their women out the streets. What is your problem? Never mind don't even answer

*that, you can start eating, I'm going wake Malakhi up for breakfast."
I walked off before he could respond.*

*I would love to say we had the perfect relationship but then I
would be a liar. Prez had started coming in later and later. We were
past the point of having to be in traps, that's what the workers were
for; so, I don't know why he would rather be there than at home with
his family. I cooked, cleaned, took amazing care of our son, sucked
the skin off his dick without being asked, and fucked that nigga in a
coma sometimes twice a day.*

*Pushing that to the back of my mind, I walked into my son's
room. I smiled at the décor. Knowing we were raising a prince, his
room's theme was royalty. The colors were a powder blue and gold
with little crown accents. Everything was perfectly place in his room
with one exception.*

*I ran from Malakhi's room to mine and back in the dining
room where Prez was feeding his face without a care in the world.*

*"Prez, I've told you one too many times to let me know when
your mom takes Malakhi. You had me worried sick! Why would you
even let me run upstairs if you knew he was gone?" I fussed until I
saw a strange look cross his face.*

*"Dynastii, the fuck is you talking about son, my mama still on
her cruise. Khi should be in his room," he said, causing my heart to
skip a beat as I ran back up the stairs to confirm what I already knew;
my son was missing.*

*"Prez, my fucking child is missing!" were the last words that
fell from my lips as I collapsed.*

***

Waking up in a cold sweat I couldn't stop the tears from
falling from my eyes, the dream felt as if it had just happened
for the first time. Climbing out of the bed, I made my way across
the hall to Malakhi's room and grabbed his blanket. Sinking to
the floor, I rocked back and forth thinking of my son. It had been
twenty-one days since he had gone missing and just ten days

since his body was left on my doorstep in a car seat. I've never known hurt like this, my child, my heart; my life was taken from me. I had never felt so disrespected, someone came in my house and snatched my heart out of his crib then returned his body back to me, and I was left with the aftermath. I blamed myself from the moment he was kidnapped. I cried for him to be returned, I begged God to give me back my baby no matter the circumstances. I didn't know those circumstances would be in death. I didn't know I was crying until I felt Prez lifting me up from the ground.

"I just want my baby, President! I just want my baby! You did this. I know you did! Who are you beefing with! You are the reason Malakhi is gone! I want some fucking answers! I've noticed that you came home with blood on your clothing twice! Did you find them and you aren't saying something who is it?" I screamed as he carried me to the walk-in shower, we were both already naked so he walked in with my legs wrapped around his waist.

"I just want my baby! I just want my baby!" I cried over and over, as he took his time washing me then himself. After he dried me off, he laid me in the bed and walked out of the room. I didn't realize I fell asleep until I woke up with Traci, Prez's mom in my face.

"Let me do something to your hair Dynastii, we only have a couple of hours before the funeral." I saw the concern in her eyes, in everyone's eyes when they looked at me. They could keep the fucking pity and the bullshit meals they had been dropping off; I just wanted my fucking son.

"Where is Mizanii and Serenity? They were supposed to bring me over something to wear," I said in a voice I didn't recognize. Waking up from your sleep screaming for weeks tend to steal your voice from you.

"They're in the guess room getting ready. Can I get anything for you?" she asked.

"Yes," I paused as I climbed out of the bed and headed to the bathroom, "Malakhi. If anyone wants to get me anything, they can bring me my son, alive and happy. The way I left him in his crib before someone decided to disrespect me and my home and take him. Other than that, I want to be left alone. I can dress myself."

Slamming the bathroom door behind me I finally looked in the mirror and shook my head at the sight before me. I saw the weight loss in my face and the bags under my eyes was proof of the restless nights I've been having. After handling my business, I walked back into my now empty room and prepared for the third worst day of my life. I didn't think I could make it through the day my son went missing and I did, then when his body was delivered back to us I thought the coroner would have to take me too. But how do I walk out of the graveyard knowing my baby wasn't coming home with me? Looking at the attire that was set out for me, I knew that Mizanii picked it out. She was a fashionista and any chance she got she would play dress up with me. I slipped on the clothing and got down on my knees to talk with God.

"Lord, please wrap your arms around me on today. I know you have your reasons but I can't understand why you would take my Malakhi. I needed him, I still need him, and I will always need him. I feel like I can't breathe without him here and everyone says I should trust you because you don't make mistakes, but I can't help but feel like you may have made your first one. I am but a shell of a woman with him. He was my reason to get up and do better. He made me better and I fear that him being gone may cause hell here on Earth for a lot of people. I changed for the better with him here and I pray you can help me to stay on this path. Just help me make it through this day. And more importantly watch over my baby boy."

Wiping the single tear that fell from my eye I stood and bumped into Prez in his all black suit. I turned to the floor length mirror and brushed my blonde hair into a high bun as he stared at my reflection.

"The car is here to pick us up," he finally spoke.

"I'll be ready in a bit," I mumbled.

"This morning was completely uncalled for; I'm hurting seeing you hurt. Don't accuse me of having shit to do with Malakhi's death ever again, Dynastii. I'm combing the streets to make sure these niggas are dealt with. He's in a better place, ma."

Grabbing my Chloe shades, I slid them on and headed for the door without saying a word before spinning around. "Your ass should be hurting because your son is gone, not because I'm hurting. For once fucking call him your son! And don't tell me no shit about him being in a better place. There's no better place for Khi than with me, his motherfucking momma!"

Through the whole funeral service, Prez gave me my space as I silently mourned for my son. I guess that's something I still carried from the streets, show no emotion. It was fine to break down in the comforts of my home but for some reason the tears stayed at bae until we made it to the graveyard. Just as my son's body was being lowered, my world shattered yet again.

"Are you President Pierre?" I heard from behind me and spun around face to face with about six cops who had their eyes trained on Prez.

Chapter 1:

Dynastii

4 months later

Sitting in the backseat of the Tahoe I was able to be alone with my thoughts even though I wasn't alone. On the outside, I looked calm, cool, and collected all the while, I was dying a thousand deaths. How did my life go from damn near perfect straight to hell? That question ran through my mind the entire two-hour drive to visit Prez. After ignoring calls and burning his letters, I was finally able to pull it together enough to go and see him. I had a million thoughts running through my head. At the top of that list was who was it that he killed? Why was he arrested? Did Prez find out what happened to my son? I needed to know that more than anything.

"Sis we're here," Mizanii said from the driver seat snapping me from my thoughts.

Climbing out of the car, I adjusted my clothing and started the process of being searched for visitation. It wasn't long before I watched Prez make his way to me. Prison had definitely done his body well; the weight he put on was pure muscle. For the first time in forever, I felt a smile spread across my face that I couldn't help.

"Damn, a nigga must be dreaming," he said, pulling me to my feet and wrapping his arms around me. "On the cool I don't want to let you go, there's no telling when I'll get the chance to hold you again." I stayed wrapped up in his arms as he inhaled my scent.

"You're so extra Prez, I ain't going nowhere," I said, pulling away and taking a seat.

"You sure could have fooled me. I ain't lying I thought you gave up on me, ma. This jail shit, I can do anything they throw at me with no problem. I can handle being here, but a nigga was suffocating without you. I can't handle losing you Dynastii. You are my whole world and then some. I know you hurting ma but I need you in my corner, I need you to be my rider again. Stop ignoring my damn calls and write me back. And I know your ass knew that would be me facetiming you." He mugged me.

"Man, I just needed time. Everything that could go wrong in my life did, all at the same fucking time too. Do you know that I haven't stepped foot in our house since we left... the morning they took you? I couldn't bring myself to speak on the funeral aloud. "Without you and... the house just ain't a home if I have to be there by myself." I knew I couldn't mention my baby without crying, so I didn't.

"Look ma, I know it's goin' be hard so I ain't even about to make you discuss that. How has school been going?" I looked down at my lap before answering him.

"I dropped out," I mumbled.

"Don't be ashamed ma, school ain't for everybody. You're going through some shit so maybe that was for the best." I lifted my eyes and met his as he finished that statement.

"I'm going back though!" I felt the need to say.

"Yeah, alright. So, what you doing now?" he asked, looking around the visiting room.

"Prez, I don't know what I'm doing. I'm out here lost. A bitch feels like she may snap at any given moment. I'm doing just enough to get by these days. You don't know how pissed off I get when I wake up in the morning. I'm really sitting here welcoming death at this point. I have so much anger inside of me I swear I already feel sorry for the next person that pisses me off. I have bond money set to the side for that day because

I can feel it coming. I feel like if a bitch gives me cold fries in the drive thru that's her ass! The old Dynastii's coming out and I don't know how to control that shit. I don't know if I want to control that shit. I hear everybody whispering about how I lost it and all I really want to say is no I found it. That monster that I buried a while back, I found it again. Why did you have to do me that, Prez? Why you left me out here naked? You're my shelter when it's storming and without you, I'm that same homeless ass kid you met way back in the gap. When everyone turned their back on me, you were supposed to still be here and what do I have now? A facetime call here and there, a letter every week, a fucking forty-five-minute supervised visit. You want to know why I couldn't answer those calls, or write you back, or come visit? It's because of the way I'm feeling now! I'm looking at that clock on the wall and I know in thirty bitch ass minutes they going tell me it's time to go and leave my world trapped here. When I see you facetiming me I can't answer because I know it's short lived as the fuck. I don't want to deal with having to see your face and faking like I'm happy when I know my pillow goin' be soaked with tears. Reading a letter from you will have me scared to flip the page knowing that it may end in the next few sentences. I've never feared the words *"love you always"* until I realized they would symbolize you telling me bye, again. I love my son dearly and I still hurt over saying bye to him that one time, do you know what it would do to my soul to tell you bye over and over and over again? Can you imagine that? I just want the pain to stop President; I can't live like this much longer," I confessed, wiping the silent tears that fell down my face. I felt a little of the weight lift from my shoulders after getting that off my chest. What I didn't expect was his next words.

"You're inconsiderate as the fuck, Dy. Why the fuck would you bring your ass down here saying that shit knowing it would make my time harder in here. Man, I've never seen you so fucking broken in my life and that shit pissing me off. You ain't no weak bitch so don't start acting like one now. So, you're telling me all this to say what? You want out because a nigga locked up. I never pegged you as one of those bitches. I fucking took care of you when you didn't have shit and this how you trying to move? I'm going beat this case then I'm goin' get out and find the niggas responsible for Malakhi's death—"

"Wait, that's not who you're in here for?" I interrupted.

"Nah."

The laugh that left my lips was damn near satanic.

"Next time you come out of your right mind and disrespect me that Dynastii you want to come out so bad will fucking appear. Nigga, that bitch word looked real fucking comfortable coming out your mouth, make it your last time. And a bitch might be bruised but I damn sure ain't broken. Yeah, they took it out of me by killing my baby, but remember Dynastii does everything but fold! If for one moment I thought I wanted to leave you then I would and it ain't shit you could do about it, nigga! And since you being disrespectful let me top that shit, a real man wouldn't have made a move until he found his son's killers. I would have had their head on a silver platter before my son's casket was picked out! It's cool, momma got Malakhi. You enjoy your comfort cause I'm goin' cause hell!" I stood up from the table shaking I was so pissed off!

"Dynastii! Dynastii! Let that shit rock until I handle it! Don't do nothing stupid!" I heard him screaming from behind me. I didn't even bother to look back. He wanted the Dynastii that was a problem then fuck it, let's do math.

***

"Y'all wait in the car, I'm good just let me rock for a second," I told Serenity and Mizanii as I stepped out of the car.

I kicked off my heels and held them in my hands as I made my way through the freshly cut grass. With every step, it felt like my legs got heavier making it harder and harder to walk. Laying down the blanket I brought with me, I sat Indian style and just stared for a moment.

"Hey baby boy, mama doesn't really know how this works. Do I just think about what I want to say, or do I say it aloud? I need a lil' help because I feel crazy just sitting here talking out loud." I chuckled.

"I've found that whatever helps you release whatever you're feeling is the best thing to do. Sometimes I sit silently and just enjoy my brother's presence. Sometimes I curse him out for leaving without saying bye. On today I wanted to sip and chill with my lil' nigga so here I am," the stranger said holding up a bottle of Hennessey. "If we were in a different place I would ask how you were doing but since we are where we are my name is Amir, nice to meet you."

I reached out to shake the hand that he extended and felt something. I couldn't place a name to the something but I know that I felt something. Looking in his eyes I know he felt it too.

"My name is Dynastii. And that's my hand you're still holding." I chuckled. I watched him look down at my ring.

"You shouldn't be sad, beautiful. My aunt B always told me that to be absent from the body is to be present with the Lord. I know that there's no better place for your son to be other than with you, but God always has a method to his madness."

My mouth fell slightly open as I stared at this stranger. How is it that he understood my situation better than the man who knew me for six years?

"Well thank your Aunt B for that bit of advice. Umm, my hand..." I reminded him again that he was still holding it.

"I've never been one to bite my tongue sweetheart so I'll just say my piece and move on. I'm fully aware that I'm still holding your hand, when we touched it just felt right. The only reason I'm letting you go without putting up a fight is because I would never step on your fiancé's toes. At least now, I have something new to tell my brother. I can tell him about the girl that got away," he said, disappointing me by letting my hand go.

"Fiancé? Oh, this isn't an engagement ring," I said giggling. "Yes, I am in a relationship but I'm not engaged yet."

"Oh, so the ring is to let people know you're off limits? Why not just propose if you're spending that type of money on a Micro pave Diamond ring?" For the first time, I was embarrassed to admit.

"It's a promise ring. Just for now, we'll get married… later. How did you know what kind of ring this was?" I curiously asked.

"I am obsessed with all things diamond; if I don't know anything else I know jewelry. And later means… When he's left the game? From me to you pretty lady a real man can be involved in any criminal ring you can name and still keep his family safe. Changing your lady's last name will do nothing but let the world know that she's your queen and show her you're serious about the relationship. I'll let you visit your son, enjoy the rest of your day beautiful."

Just like that he walked away from me. I watched as he made his was further down the row of graves before taking a seat on the grass with his back facing me. The cologne he wore still tickled my nose and for a second I forgot where I was and why. Sitting back down I shook my head at myself.

"Baby, let's keep this lil' conversation between you and me but for a moment I forgot about your father." I genuinely laughed for the first time in months. "Momma is missing you like crazy. I'm sorry this is my first time coming here but it's really hard baby. I promise to come more often; you have my word. I need you to put in a word for me, ask God to watch over me and forgive me in advance for what I'm about to do. Momma needs some answers and I will get them. I brought these for you so you wouldn't be bored," I said, pulling out the toy trains and placing them on his grave. "I would have brought your favorite bear but he helps mommy sleep at night, maybe we could share him for now. I have to go now but always remember that I love you past infinity." I leaned forward and kissed the picture of him that was attached to his tombstone before folding my blanket and making it back to the car.

"How are you feeling, sis?" Mizanii asked once I closed the door.

"You know what, Z I'm feeling better than I have in ages." I smiled.

"It wouldn't have anything to do with tall, dark, and handsome man that held your hand for hours, huh?" she asked as her and Serenity burst out laughing.

"I ain't thinking about that man, but I do have a proposition for the both of you. First thing first, let's go shopping. I need something new. A complete makeover and Mizanii I'm completely following your lead," I said as we pulled off. I was getting answers sooner rather than later and I feel sorry for the bitch niggas that violated me in the worst way.

Chapter 2:

Tec

Seeing the matte black Benz parked in my circular drive-way immediately pissed me off. Pulling out my cell phone, I called my nigga Sage.

"Yo, I was just about to hit you up," he answered.

"Bet. Aye, I need you to come to my spot ASAP and take all Ashanti's information out of my damn systems."

"Tec, you know like I know her ass only there because you never told her that she couldn't be there. You know if you say the word, she wouldn't bother you anymore. That girl got you wrapped around her wrinkled ass fingers." He laughed.

"Nobody asked you all that shit, Dr. Phil. Bring your ass around here before I put hands on her retarded ass," I said, hopping out of my car and walking up to my front door while saying a silent prayer.

Walking through the downstairs portion of the house, I didn't see Ashanti and knew exactly where she was. The ringing of my phone halted my journey up the stairs.

"Good Afternoon Aunt B," I answered.

"Hey baby, Sage was just here so I know that nappy headed hoe [BJ3]is over there. You need me to come over there and pull an Amora?" she confused me.

"Aunt B, what's an Amora?"

"You know she's forever telling someone she going snatch their ass. Let me know because I will fuck that bitch up and make it back in time for bible study!" she said, causing me to chuckle. My Aunt Betty, or B as we all call her, swears she's saved but curses like a sailor and always wants to fight somebody.

"You're a trip but no I got it. I'm just going kick her ass out," I said.

"Amir Jaquees Coleman, watch your damn mouth when you're on the phone with me!" she snapped like she wasn't just cursing up a storm.

"My bad, let me get her out my crib so I can shower and go meet these people," I quickly attempted to end the call.

"Yeah right, you just make sure you don't put your hands on that girl. I didn't raise you to do that but give me a call and Amora and I are in route!" she said, hanging up. I smelled her perfume before I could fully make it in my bedroom. Removing my shoes, I placed them next to her red bottoms at the door. Sitting on my bed, I listened to the conversation she was having from my bathroom.

"He's doing fine but he misses his daddy," I heard her say followed by a chuckle then silence and I assumed the person was talking. "No baby, I have everything handled. Facetime me tonight and I'll let y'all speak. He woke up this morning asking for you and of course, I told him you were working. He'll be happy to see you," she spoke again followed by more silence then, "I love you more. Bye daddy." She finished.

I listened to the sound of the jets in the bathtub as I thought back on how Ashanti and I got to this place we were in.

Ashanti was the love of my life and had been so since our middle school years. When she moved on our block all the niggas wanted her but she gave none of us play, not even me. For months on end, I was trying to win her over. I used my allowance to buy her flowers and lil' cheap ass gifts and she ate that shit up, each time still turning me down. She was first and only chick I loved. We didn't get together until I was in high school,

I should have seen her for what she was then. She didn't pay me any attention until I got a lil' name for myself in the streets. I spoiled her and I know I'm to blame for the brat she is today. She wouldn't cook, clean, or fuck me but she damn sure knew how to say, "Give me some money" in every damn language. I even tolerated that until she did the unthinkable.

"Baby, I didn't know you were home." Ashanti's vice pulled me from my thoughts.

"Ashanti, what the fuck are you doing in my house, again?" I asked looking over at her dripping wet body. There was no denying that my ex-fiancée was one of the sexiest women I laid eyes on. She was dancing on the line of being thick and a BBW, but she had the tiniest waistline. Her red complexion was still blemish and stretch mark free. She was doing this whole natural thing with her hair, but it wasn't natural because it was actually a head full of weave. Her full lips and almond shaped eyes still drew me in after all of these years.

"Amir, did you hear what I was saying?" she said, running her hand down my face.

"Nah, get'cho hands out my face though," I said, hitting her hand away. "Now why are you in my shit?"

"I missed you and thought I would stop by and give you some of what you've been missing," she said, licking her lips.

"Fuck, I've been missing the money you stole; is that what you're bringing me? I been missing the meals I would beg for, you cooking? Because if all you brought me was pussy, you could have kept it pushing, shawty. I'm good on that," I said side eyeing her.

"Amir, how many times do you want me to apologize? I told you why I needed the money!" She had the nerve to raise her voice.

"I don't want you to apologize; I want you to run me my money. Yeah, you did tell me why you needed the money, but

I'm having trouble understanding when that became my problem."

"Why must you be an asshole when it comes to him? And you have money Amir so don't act like that shit set you back. You know you can just step in your brother's shoes and be a millionaire by now," she asked.

"Cause that lil' nigga ain't for me. And the next time you wanna shoot the shit with his daddy, do that shit at your spot not mine. And I already told your ass, I AIN'T GOING BACK TO THE STREETS! You talk as if I don't have a career. I make great money. The shit put you in the house you're staying in."

"And I appreciate it, but that's hardly enough house for Ezra and I to grow in. I'm not really concerned about that though because we'll be back here soon enough." She said with a smile.

"Ashanti, you have a fucking four bedroom, three bathroom home. What you mean that ain't enough house? You really take this ungrateful shit to another level and it fucking blows me. I gave your ass the world on a silver platter and it still wasn't enough. And as for moving back here, you can hang it up."

As usual she tried to distract me by unzipping my pants and trying to free my dick. I hate to say that it was working.

"Don't say you don't want pussy cause we both know you don't casually fuck. Let me make you feel good like I used to. I know you still want me; I mean you haven't removed my fingerprint from the database. I'm sure it's because self-consciously you know we'll get back together," she whispered in my ear.

"And that's where I come in at. Ashanti, put on some damn clothes sitting over there looking like a wet ass poodle," my homie Sage said, walking in and saving the day. "I'm glad I came through; your ass was going get up with fleas messing with her ass," he said like she wasn't still standing right there. Instead of running away and putting clothes on her naked body, she decided to stand there ass naked and argue.

"Amir, when are you going to make him show me some respect?" she asked standing with her legs spread apart and hands on her hips.

"Shit, when you show me something to respect. Go put on some fucking clothes," he said, looking at her with disgust.

"This is why I'm changing my codes. Even with me standing here your ass is still eye fucking my nigga. And go get dressed, disrespectful ass bitch," I said, pushing her in the back of her head towards the bathroom.

"Look like I came just in time, huh?" He laughed dabbin' me up.

"Right, I knew I kept your ass around for a reason. As soon as her funky ass gets out of my bathroom, you can change around all that shit. I'm glad I changed my safe combination. The bitch can act like she ain't touched it, but I know I had my shit stacked against it." I nodded towards the safe that was now in clear view.

"You do know I can hear you right, Amir?" she asked, walking out of the bathroom dressed like she was heading to a club. The funny part is this was her everyday attire. She was always dressed like a rich thot.

"You do know I'm not whispering, right? Ashanti, get the fuck out my shit before I get you out shawty," I said, waving her off as Sage began laughing.

"Sage that's why your white ass can't find a bitch, you're always in me and mines business!" she snapped.

"And that's why you can't find a baby daddy, you always trying to suck a nigga dick. Fuck outta here Ashanti with that dehydrated weave."

Those words touched a nigga soul. When Ashanti told me she was pregnant, I immediately found a house that I thought

I would be starting my family in. Against my aunt B's wishes I proposed to her ass because I wanted to do things right. I wanted my child to have both parents and grow up in a loving home. My parade was rained on when she was running her mouth in the salon and it got back to me that she was carrying some other nigga's seed. Of course, she lied until I told her who my source was, my sister Amora. She came clean and begged for me to forgive her. Like I said I've loved her since middle school so I tried to make it work. I even bonded with her son. I refused to sign the birth certificate and called off the wedding until I could wrap my head around the situation. I helped raise lil' man until he made around ten months. That's when I found out she was still communicating with his father. She even had that nigga thinking they were together, like what the fuck was I here for then? I cut all ties with her and her kid, it hurt more losing him then it did losing her.

"I know who my child's father is, thank you!" she said, grabbing her heels from the door. "Amir, can I have some money for my bills?" she asked with her hand out.

"Didn't you just say you knew who the child's father was? Ask that nigga!" I snapped. I watched as tears pooled around her eyes.

"Why you have to be so cold towards me, Amir? I fucked up; it was a mistake I regret every day of my life. Do I have to get punished repeatedly for the same thing?" she said, letting the tears fall.

"You better not fall for those thot tears," Sage said.

Knowing I should have just kicked her ass out and got rid of her for good I went in my pocket and handed her all the cash I had, about two stacks.

"You better make it fucking stretch. Call up to the store Monday; I'll have them set you up with some work," I said as she turned up her nose.

"Work!" she shrieked. "I haven't worked a day of my life. Why do I need a job?"

"And that's your fucking problem now—" Sage started before I cut him off.

"Sage! Nigga, I got this. Go take your ass and start changing my shit." I laughed as his childish ass flicked Ashanti off. "You better not let this poodle have you in here listening to sad ass songs later or I swear I'll put you out of your misery," he said, tapping his hip where I know his gun was. Sage was knee deep in the streets and had no intentions on leaving.

"I really hate him, Amir. Why do you hang around with him?" she asked as if she had the privilege of getting an answer.

"You won't have to worry about that, because you won't be around to see him. Bye Ashanti." I nudged her towards the door and followed her out.

"You're not going ask how Ezra is doing?" she asked me.

"Nope, not my concern," I said, opening the front door.

When she saw Sage standing there messing with the system she immediately sucked her teeth before she went flying across the porch. For a second I thought she tripped over her high ass heels until I heard laughter. "Sage did you trip that girl?" I asked helping her up.

"They said bitches stay falling for me," he replied, laughing as Ashanti attempted to get at him.

"Laugh now Sage, you will get what's coming to you," she threatened before hoping in her car and pulling off.

"Nigga, why are you so mean to that girl?" I asked, laughing.

"Because I can't stand her ass and the way she played my brother." He said imitating ole girl from the movie, *Save the Last Dance*. "Nah but on the real, that hoe doesn't sit right with me. Something ain't right about her," he said seriously.

"Respect," I answered.

"What you getting into tonight?" I asked

"I got a lil' sit down with some new people that's trying to get put on, wanna come feel them out for old time's sake?" he asked, causing me to think it over.

"Yeah, I ain't got shit else to do."

Chapter 3:

Dynastii

"Zaaaammmmmmnnnn, Dy! Bitch you know that ass is way too fat for those tight ass shorts," Mizanii said as I walked to the living room and modeled for them. The tight denim True Religion shorts were struggling to conceal my shapely ass and hips.

"What, I think I look like a typical around the way thot," I said as I looked at my attire in the floor length mirror. The red *"trust no bitch"* muscle shirt was a size too small but that didn't stop me from wearing it. The decision to go bra-less left my nipple piercings on display just as planned. I topped my fit with a pair of red and white 6's. "Don't act like this wasn't something I would wear way back in the gap. This is what had Prez going crazy," I said, bending forward and making my ass clap.

"Nah, it was your ass going crazy. Remember we pulled up on Prez and No Legz chilling with some hoes. Your ass didn't know which one was entertaining Prez so you whipped both of their asses," Mizanii said, laughing as I fingered through my now black tresses. I remembered that day all too well, it ended in Prez fucking all our beef away as usual.

"One of the many times I checked a bitch instead of my nigga. I learned my lesson about that shit a long time ago though, and I've been running in Prez's shit since. That nigga had my head gone."

"I told you long time ago to leave that nigga." Mizanii never cared much for Prez and the way he used to treat me.

"Well the heart wants what it wants. Besides, I don't get in your business with your plethora of men so stay out of mine.

Y'all ready to go?" I asked, checking out their attire.

Mizanii was killing a denim romper that hugged her curves and a pair of gold metallic Puma's by Rihanna. Serenity completed off the trio rocking a tight pair of distressed white Seven jeans, a red crop top shirt that had her huge titties praying to be freed and a pair of custom red Yeezy boost. Pressing the push to start button on my brand-new candy red Benz, I sped off blasting the perfect song for the occasion, Lil' Kim's "Big Momma Thang". Thirty minutes later, I found myself posted up on the hood of my whip on one of the busiest blocks.

"Can I wash your car for some spare change?" asked what I knew to be a crackhead.

"Nah, my baby just got washed, she's straight." I waved him off and grabbed the blunt that Serenity was passing to me.

"So, what are we waiting out here for again?" Mizanii asked, sliding the oversized shades on her head.

"For word to get around that we're sitting here, these niggas ain't even checking their surroundings. We aren't regular faces and they should have been here to see why the fuck we chilling here," I said, kissing my teeth. If I were still running the streets with Prez this type of laziness wouldn't have been tolerated.

"You can take the girl out the hood..." Mizanii said, laughing.

If anyone knew how deep this street shit ran for me my lil' sister did. She and Serenity had seen me in action more times than I could count. When they started talking about being down, I taught them all that I knew and used them to assist me from time to time. Though Serenity wasn't my biological sister, blood couldn't make us any closer. We had a history that would forever bond us. After twenty minutes and another blunt of sitting down, I grew impatient.

"Nah fuck that, let's go to their asses," I said, jumping

down from my car and hitting the locks. Walking over to the biggest house on the block, I had to laugh at how creative they were. The house looked as if an older couple would live here. There were two rocking chairs on the porch, a flowerbed that was in full bloom, wind chimes, and even a damn welcome mat. If I didn't know what I knew I would be convinced that this wasn't a trap house. Fixing my shorts as I hopped on the porch I knocked on the door and waited.

"Put the fucking controller down and answer the door, nigga!" I heard a deep voice bark from somewhere near the front of the house. Hearing footsteps approaching the door I took a step back and waited.

"Damn, who the fuck y'all here for?" asked the ugliest man I had ever seen. I had seen my fair share of ugly men but nothing topped this one. He had his Fatty Wap shit going on with one eye, nappy dreads that hadn't been twisted in years, and the ashiest skin I had ever seen.

"Not you, where is Prez at?" I asked in the most ratchet voice I could muster. I'm talking popping gum and everything.

"What you looking for Prez for?" he asked.

"Well, I copped some weed from one of his people and I want what I paid for or I want my money back! I paid for some Kush and got this bitch ass Reggie," I said, getting louder than necessary.

"Get the fuck out of here; we don't even fuck with Reggie around here. You got the wrong people, shorty."

"Look, I know we got it from Prez people because that's the only nigga we fuck with. It's obvious I'm talking to an employee when what I'm really looking for is a boss. So, do me a favor and get me whoever is in charge here!" Mizanii snapped. I don't even think he heard because he was too busy eyeing the way her full lips sucked on the sucker that was in her mouth.

"Black, who the fuck is at the door." I heard from inside

before a much more doable face presented itself. Laying it on thick, I made eye contact with him and licked my lips.

"Can you get me whoever is running this house please?" I pouted.

"Shit, I run this house? Wassup with you?" he asked as I *accidently* dropped the bag of weed from my back pocket onto the ground. Turning around I bent over so that they got an eyeful of the ass spilling from my shorts.

"I thought Prez ran this house? I always deal with him."

"Nah baby girl, there's a new boss in town. What can I help you with?" he said, stepping out the front door.

"Look, I got some Reggie when I really wanted some Kush. I paid for Kush actually. Can you fix their fuck up since you're in charge?" I asked, stepping closer to him.

"Ma, that ain't even our packaging." He pulled out a small Ziploc bag showcasing the skeleton head on the front. "All our shit is branded. Now if you want to get you some Kush then I damn sure can get you right." I noticed the double meaning and had to force myself not to smirk at his dumb ass.

"Well we actually used to work out deals with Prez, if you know what I mean. Call him and let him know his favorite sisters are waiting for him," Mizanii answered sucking on that damn sucker harder than necessary.

"Shit y'all don't need to work shit out with him. That nigga's facing football numbers, so I'm who y'all need to see. I'm running shit from now on so I don't even want to hear his name mentioned around these parts. Let's just say the president has been impeached. My name Polo, and that's all I wanna hear you scream from this point forward. Y'all can come in and show me why y'all were his favorite sisters though. Like I said I'll get y'all right," he said, grabbing my hand and leading me inside.

"Shit, can I have you then? I can hook you up too," Lil' ugly said to Serenity who played her role as a shy girl.

"Oh nah, she ain't part of the deal. She's a virgin and I wanna keep it that way," I said, watching his one eye shine with excitement.

"Shit, I'm a virgin too." He laughed but I believed him. The sight of his ugly ass made my pussy go dry, so I can't imagine who would let him fuck. "We ain't gotta do nothing she ain't cool with," he said, grabbing Serenity's hand as she lightly blushed.

"It's cool sis, I actually wanna chill with his cute ass. I heard y'all were playing the game, y'all better have 2K," she said

"Shit we can do that too, let's go," he said, pulling her to the front as we walked to the back of the house with Polo.

Walking in the room, I was shocked the house was actually spotless. In the back of the room, I heard a money machine going and directed my attention to the nigga working it. He stared at me for a second before looking at Polo.

"Say Polo what's this, you know we don't bring bitches in the spot," he said.

"Nigga chill, we about to have a lil' fun. You gotta bounce. Let the fiends know the spot closed until I'm finished here," he said, dismissing ole dude.

I watched as Polo walked over to the closet and fumbled around for a moment then walked back in front of the bed. Quickly, he placed his phone, keys, and his gun on the nightstand then removed his clothes. With only his boxers on, he laid back in the bed.

"Damn you move fast, you goin' give us what we came for, right?" I asked in the same ghetto voice.

"Shit, that and some shit you never knew you needed. Y'all take off those clothes, slowly," he said, pulling out his dick and stroking it. The licking of my lips this time wasn't forced; his dick was a work of art. It was long and thick enough to do some serious damage, and that curve was an added bonus. "You ain't know I nigga was carrying like this, huh?"

"Oh, I'm taking a ride on that," Mizanii said, staring at his dick hungrily. My sister was a certified nympho so I know her saying that wasn't part of the act. She was serious. Slowly removing our clothing, we were left in just our lace thongs.

"Damn, you got your nipples pierced ma? That shit is sexy as the fuck. Why don't you have a piercing?" he asked, looking from my nipples to Mizanii's.

"Oh, I got a piercing," she said, sliding off her thong and holding her right leg up by her ankle. Polo damn near started drooling when he saw her clit was pierced. With one finger, he motioned for us to come near him and that midget leg he called a dick.

"If we do this, you can't tell nobody," I naively said.

"Shit, don't worry about that. From this point forward, y'all are both for me. Shit, I got enough dick to handle both of y'all thick asses. I'll keep y'all supplied if y'all keep a nigga nuts empty." He laughed at his own corny joke.

"You got a condom?" I looked at Mizanii and almost burst out laughing because she was still sucking on the sucker. Grabbing the magnum from his extended hand, she tore the wrapper with her teeth then slowly slid it on his throbbing dick.

"Say shorty bring that pussy here so I can get it wet for you to ride," he said to her.

"Nah boo, I got this. She stays wet don't you worry." Standing on the bed, she lowered her body until she had completely sunk down on his dick. "Hold this down for me," she said removing the sucker she had been sucking on and popped it in his mouth. I stifled a laugh cause his dumb ass didn't remove it. I watched as she slowly started grinding on him and his eyes rolled to the back of his head. I was in a relationship so I knew I wasn't fucking him, but a lil' head was harmless. At least that's what Prez said the last time he was caught cheating. Pulling off my thong, I removed the sucker from his lip and sat on his face. I was enjoying my ride until this nigga literally started eating my pussy. Feeling his teeth on my pussy damn near trying to take a bite caused me to hop off his face.

"Nah baby, this ain't Chinese food. Just stick your tongue out and let me do the rest." I said. When I noticed he followed my directions I took my seat once again and rode his tongue until all my juices were spilling over. Mizanii's loud moans let me know that she was getting hers too.

"Shit, if you ride a tongue like that, let me see how you ride a dick," Polo said as Mizanii's shaking subsided. I watched as she climbed down from his semi erect dick.

"Nah daddy, I'm not the regular girl. Normal things don't make me nut," I said, licking my lips.

"Yeah, what you like anal?" He smirked.

"Nope, blood," I said, smirking back.

"Blood?" was the last words he got out before I shot him in both kneecaps with the gun I had dropped on side of the bed. I listened for footsteps but was confident that because of the silencer and the fact that Serenity had the television turned up, they weren't coming.

"Nigga if you scream I'll bust your head wide the fuck open, with your own shit!" I spat. "Z, take care of that nigga in the front," I ordered. Mizanii's silly ass skipped out of the room but ass naked.

"Bitch who the fuck sent you to run through my shit?" he asked, making me laugh.

"Didn't I tell your ass Prez ran this shit? You're real cocky when I know your ass ain't shit but a bitch boy. You know why Heat got ghost so easily? That nigga knew exactly who I was. See fucking with Prez's money is like fucking with mine, hell it is fucking with mine. Let me tell you where you fucked up at. One, you niggas slacking, I was up front too long with no one checking out the scene. Two, you let me come up in your spot, with money and product back there. Three, you closed up shop like your ass is really running shit. Four, nigga you bit my pussy. And five, don't ever disrespect my man."

"Your man? Who the fuck is your man? Who the fuck is you?" he asked still moaning like a bitch.

"If my nigga is the president to the streets, then I'm known as the first lady to the streets. And the two bitches I rolled in here with are the heads of security." I finished shooting him right between the eyes and instantly ending his life.

"Damn, that shit was pretty," Serenity said, getting hype. I laughed as Mizanii came back in the room wiping blood from her arms.

"Bitch, why are you still naked and full of blood?" I had to ask.

"You know her ass had to play with those knives instead of just shooting the nigga," Serenity said, shaking her head. I had a passion for guns but Mizanii had always been obsessed with slicing a bitch. She started with razors in her mouth then quickly upgraded to blades. If she pulled one out, run!

"Shit, I had to re-pop my cherry; it's been a while since I caught a body." She laughed as she slid on her clothes. That dick was A1 though," she said, looking at a very dead Polo.

"I didn't tell you to fuck the nigga," I said.

"Shit, I don't need permission to pop my pussy!" she replied. Remembering that Polo played in the closet, I opened the door to see a camera pointing at the bed, recording.

"Oooh you know I like to watch myself, give me that tape," Mizanii said so I tossed the whole camera her way. "So, what's next?" she asked.

"Re-up. I already set up a sit down with the plug."

Chapter 4:

Tec

"Do you really have to do all that extra shit for a sit down? You always gotta be a pretty boy," Sage said as I lined my beard up.

"Sage, my nigga, you have two houses. Why are you always in my shit?" I asked, looking at him through the mirror. "And where the fuck is your clothes at?"

"I had to wash my ass just like you had to wash yours. How you snap at me and your ass walking around in less than me. At least I have on basketball shorts and a muscle shirt, you sitting here in boxers. You put on some fucking clothes!"

"When I fell asleep yo ass had already left, so why are you back at my spot?"

"You shouldn't have let me programmed your spot. Now I have full access whenever I want to," he said, walking out my room.

Sage was my brother from another mother. If no one else had my back, he did. I met him back in middle school when we were trying out for the football team. The other dudes were clowning him because he was trying out in the same dirty Nikes that he wore to school daily, while we all had new cleats. The fact that he was wearing the same jeans and t-shirts that he would wear to school every day seemed so irrelevant after his mom showed up. They laughed him off the field when they saw the condition she was in, begging and crying for his lunch money. It was obvious that his mom was a crackhead. That night I couldn't get him off my mind and I'll never forget the conversation I had while sitting at the table with my aunt B, brother, and sister.

"Aunt B, why did you let us come live with you if no one else did?" I asked over dinner.

"Because I love y'all," she said with no hesitation.

"So, my daddy didn't love us?" I asked.

"I won't say that. I will just say he loves you differently than I do. Your mother is... sick, so I stepped in to help her until she gets better." She smiled as she made sure a five-year-old Amora finished her food instead of feeding the dog.

"She doesn't have a cold or the flu, so she's not sick. Mom is just a crackhead," Ahmad said with a mouth full of baked ziti.

"No, she's not Ahmad. Shut up! I saw a crackhead today and mom doesn't look like her," I naively countered.

I wasn't lying our mother, Cherelle, was still drop dead gorgeous. Even with the weight loss and thinning hair, she would pull herself together and be able to grab plenty of attention. But in my heart, I already knew Ahmad was telling the truth.

"Ahmad! Go to your damn room right now!" Aunt B said, causing Amora to start crying. She was so spoiled behind Ahmad and I that anytime we got in trouble her feelings would be hurt.

"Aunt B, what is he talking about?" I asked as Ahmad stomped up the stairs and Amora followed.

"Baby, why all these questions?" she asked. "I can already tell you know the answer, you just want me to confirm it. So, tell me, what brought this up?"

"There's this kid at school, he is like we were, before you took us in. Always dirty with the same clothes on. And the kids tease him; he doesn't have a brother like me. At least when they teased us Ahmad and I would beat them up. His mom came to school today and she was like mom was before she went away. I know they are both crackheads," I said before climbing down from the chair and heading to *the staircase.*

"Amir, we will talk about this more after I wash the dishes," *she said, causing me to turn around in time to see her wipe the tears* *from her eyes.*

"It's alright Aunt B; she'll get better and come get us. But I do *want to help the boy like you did us. You can take my allowance for* *however long it takes to get him some clothes and a pair of shoes. Oh,* *and maybe some football cleats," I said, hoping she didn't say no.*

"Is that all you think he needs?" she questioned.

"I'm sure he needs more but that's all I can offer." I shrugged.

"No, you can offer him to come here after school for a few *days. I'm sure he'll appreciate the food, a good shower, and most im-* *portantly a good friend. Prepare yourself because you'll have a friend* *for life after you do all of this. And don't worry about your allow-* *ance, I'll pay for it. Now go upstairs and get ready for bed."*

"Why the fuck yo pretty ass still not dressed, bruh." Sage walked back in my room as I threw on a black Polo V-Neck over my distressed True Religion jeans. I mugged his ass as I grabbed my Movado Vizio watch and fastened it around my wrist.

"If you get the fuck out of my room, I'll grab my shoes and we can bounce," I said, grabbing a pair of Air Max from my closet. After slipping them on and a few squirts of my Versace Eros cologne we were out the door. Pulling up to the house that was solely used for meetings, I was shocked that these niggas were already there.

"At least we know they are about their business. We're twenty minutes early and they are already here, what kind of niggas are really that punctual?" I asked Sage.

"Niggas that are really bitches," he said, eyeing the three females that stepped out of the truck as soon as our feet hit the pavement. These females were all bad in a different way.

Get the fuck outta here, I whispered to myself as I pulled my

NY fitted cap further down my face. If it was one thing I knew, it was the fact that the game was no place for females. Niggas were grimy in this game and the fact that they were stepping out of the whip, hair blowing, heels sky high and face fully made up; let me know that they weren't ready for what was to come.

"Gentleman, sorry we're a little early. If you aren't ready for us we can wait out in the car for the..." she paused to check the iced-out Rolex on her wrist, "eighteen minutes," she said, cocking her head as she stared at me for a second.

"Nah y'all cool, we always ready," Sage said, unlocking the door as they walked in behind him with me following. Leading them to the dining room, we took our seats each at the head of the table. "Y'all need something to drink? I know we have soda, water probably some—" Sage started before he was cut off.

"Thanks for the offer but quick question. When niggas come through do you offer them drinks and hors d'oeuvres and shit of that sort?" asked one of the females, she carried herself like the boss so I figured she was.

"No but—" Sage started.

"But because we are females you felt the need to. Nah treat us like you treat the niggas pimp. We don't need anything to drink, what we do need however, is some work. And I have all the cash up front so I don't need any handouts. Just some of the purest shit you have at some bomb ass prices," she said, standing up with her hands on her curvaceous hips.

"It's kind of hard to consider you a nigga with that get up," he said, ignoring her request and referring to the fitted black jumpsuit thing she was wearing that flared out at the bottom.

"Nah baby I said treat us like the niggas, I'm definitely all woman. I see that and I know you damn sure see that."

"Oh, I see you. Fuck Stevie Wonder sees you; your fiancé is a lucky man," Sage flirted, eyeballing the rock that still sat on her ring finger.

"Nah she ain't engaged, that's a promise ring," I finally spoke without looking up from my phone.

"I was wondering when you were going to stop acting like you didn't know who I was, Amir, right?" Shawty from the graveyard asked.

"Now who's acting? You know fucking well you remembered my name. Dynastii, what are you really here for?" I asked, staring her down and lil' mama didn't back down.

"Oh, I told no lies; I'm here for a re-up. And make that the last time you throw shade towards my situation."

"What your lil' high school relationship?" I questioned. I watched the anger flash in her eyes before she composed herself.

"Ain't you the same nigga who was trying to wife a hoe? If my sources are correct, didn't yo bitch pop another nigga seed out of some pussy that was supposed to be yours? My shit may seem high school to you, but your shit seems like a *Maury* episode waiting to happen," she said, taking her seat again and crossing her thick thighs. The smirk on her lips is what really pissed me off.

"You shouldn't speak on what the fuck you know!" I snapped.

"And they say the game is no place for a woman cause we're too emotional, meanwhile someone has their panties in a bunch." She smiled as she fired up a blunt of what smelled like some fire.

"Damn ma, marry me!" Sage told her, getting on one knee. "That nigga's ring is nice though so let me propose to you with that shit," he said, causing a smile to spread across her face.

"Baby, nothing personal but I like my men a couple shades darker. You're cute and all, but I ain't down with the swirl. That's more of Z's thing," she said, pointing towards the chick on side of her. She was bad as fuck too; I could tell they were related.

I had to stop myself from laughing when Sage's dumb ass moved on to her as if he wasn't just trying to holla at her home girl. Clearly, she was the same boss type ass woman because before he could open his mouth she spoke.

"Run along Eminem, this pussy will ruin your life," she said before blowing smoke in his face. Not one to take anything serious he turned to the third chick, who looked to be mixed with something.

"Ma, I was saving the best for last," he said with a huge grin.

"Baby, what you have in your pants doesn't even make the pussy get moist. Shit, I like what you after, but after we do business we can go on a pussy hunt together," she said, flicking her tongue at him.

"Got damn I think I love all of y'all," Sage said really looking love struck.

"It's nice chatting with you all but I really need to get going, when will we discuss shipments?" Dynastii asked, looking down at her cell phone.

"What you have to get home to your fian... I'm sorry what do you call a fiancé that's not a fiancé?" I said. I couldn't understand where this jealousy was coming from.

"I'll tell you right after you tell me what you call the child that isn't yours," she said, staring me in the face with no hint of fear in her eyes.

Clearly if she was here she knew exactly who the fuck I was. I got my street name, Tec, because I was deadly with any guns but with a Tec 9, a nigga was a fucking problem. I had no problems leaving a whole state in mourning behind disrespect and here was this lil' ass female disrespecting me time and time again.

"Dynastii, I've killed people for a lot less than all of that shit you spitting!" I spat standing to my feet.

"And so have I, Tec, Amir, or whatever the fuck you go by; don't let the beat face fool you. Daddy, I'm a boss and will be respected as such. You give me respect and I will give you the same," She finished, standing to her feet also.

"Shit, you let that nigga disrespect you with that bullshit ass ring and excuse for not wifing you."

"And obviously being wifed up ain't shit cause yo hoe still strayed. That nigga ain't never brought home no fucking baby so check fucking mate!" she snapped back.

"Everybody get the fuck out except, Dynastii!" I roared. What pissed me off the most the fact the Sage moved before her friends, they just looked at her for orders.

"It's cool, y'all can step outside." She nodded at them never taking her eyes off of me. All that could be heard was the clicking of her home girl's heels as they made their exit.

"Sit down," I ordered.

"After you," she countered. "I never feel safe letting someone stand over me, know what I mean?"

"You're a good 5'4; I stand over you with you standing up."

"Like I said, after you," she countered again.

"What the fuck is your problem? That attitude shit ain't even cute," I said, getting pissed off.

"The only problem I have is this meeting is running over, I'm missing my new episode of *Love & Hip Hop*. And I can guarantee you, I'm not here to be cute; I'm here to make money," she answered.

"All that hot shit you were talking about my personal life is none of your fucking concern!"

"Oh, but my man is your concern?" she asked, causing me to walk around the table and get in her personal space. The fact that she didn't jump, flinch, or break eye contact was sexy as fuck.

"A man would cherish the woman he supposedly loves. A man wouldn't have his woman in a meeting with a known killer with a badass temper. A man wouldn't find some bullshit ass excuse like your nigga did for not marrying you after all these years. Shit, if a man has a queen, he crowns her ass with his last name, not continue to shuffle the deck. So, stop insulting men and calling your boy a man. You have the two confused. Cause only a high school boy gives a woman a fucking promise ring. The fuck did y'all join pinkies after he slid that on your finger? And as for getting work from me, cancel that shit! Go enroll into school or some shit like that, this is a man's game and we don't have room on our roster for your crew. We're filled to capacity," I finished while walking away. Her next statement though simple sounded like a threat.

"You sure about that? Cool." I saw the smile that didn't reach her eyes spread across her face but before I could question it she was heading towards the door.

"What the fuck happened?" Sage asked, walking back in. I looked at him for a second because his ass knew better than questioning me. Although I let Sage run the show, this was my empire. My brother, Ahmad, left it to me but a nigga didn't want this. Therefore, from time to time I would step in but for the most part this was all him.

"Don't look at me like that; you know your ass can't leave me in the dark on shit like this. I need to know if I need to watch my back because of this meeting," he said, causing me to side eye him.

"From those females?" I questioned.

"Don't act like those were some regular ass females. Those bitches were as bad as they come. Mark my words, they're gonna be a problem," he said walking out.

Chapter 5:

Mizanii

"You know we have that thing today, right?" I asked, passing the blunt and basking in the aftermath of what I had to refer to as some bomb ass sex.

"Yeah, Dynastii hit me up too," Serenity said, accepting the blunt I was handing to her.

Serenity and I had been sleeping together for as long as I can remember. She was the first and only girl I had been with and accepted the fact that we had no strings attached. She knew that while I enjoyed what we did, I needed a man in my life. Yeah, we had tons of toys, but there was nothing like a big dick with throbbing veins penetrating your pussy. No one knew about us and I planned on keeping it that way. I didn't want Dynastii to catch us so we were ducked off at an apartment she knew nothing about. Lying across Serenity's lap as she gave me an ass massage was the most relaxing moment ever.

"You think she's really goin' go through with that plan?" Serenity asked, causing me to look at her crazy.

"Now you know better than anyone, If Dy says she is going do something; then she will do it. All I know is I definitely have to watch her back because she's blinded by emotion. I want to find out who killed Khi also, but I want to be smart about it," I said.

"Yeah, and I'll watch your back while you are watching hers," Serenity said, placing soft kisses along my ass. She knew exactly how to get some shit started.

Rolling over I grabbed a handful of her hair and spread her lips with my tongue. A pet peeve of mine was a motherfucker that couldn't kiss but every time my lips touched Serenity's I was left gasping for breath. Her kiss alone was damn near orgasmic. I was so into the feeling of her lips against mine that I didn't realize she had snaked her hand across my body until I she penetrated my wet pussy with the double headed pink silicone dick that was lying in the bed. The surprise caused the loudest moan to escape my lips.

"Fuck Rin, save that love shit for the next bitch. Fuck me!" was all I needed to say before she began assaulting my pussy with her favorite toy. "Oooohhhh shit, right there baby, right fucking there!" I screamed, grabbing my hair as she punished my pussy. Rotating my hips on the dick I stared Serenity in the eyes as I felt myself about to explode.

"You cumin', mami? Come for me so I can suck you dry," she said, causing a chain reaction. My body immediately started shaking and I felt like my soul damn near leave my body as I began squirting all over. Replacing the toy with her mouth, Serenity did as she promised and sucked on my already sensitive clit. My body was still shaking from the mind-blowing orgasm when I felt her tongue penetrate my pussy. The slurping sound as well as the way she was rotating her tongue sent me over the edge once again.

"Ohhhhh... Rin... Fuck!" I said, trying to get away from her monster of a tongue. Releasing me, she came forward and attacked my lips, allowing me to taste my own juices. "Awwww," I moaned when she pulled away.

"You're such a freak. You don't even care that I stopped kissing you, you only like to taste yourself," she busted me. "I'll take a rain check on my turn, it's getting late," She said getting out of the bed and heading to the shower.

***

"You sure about this, Dy?" Serenity asked, causing Dynastii and I to stare her down.

"Look Serenity, this your what fourth time asking me if I was sure? Let me put it to you this way, I'm sure I'm walking in here. I'm even more sure I'm walking out of here, untouched. And so is Mizanii, cause we're made for this shit. The only thing I'm unsure about is you right now, to be honest," Dynastii said never taking her eyes off the front door.

"Dy, don't even insult me," Serenity said, looking hurt.

"No baby girl, I'm not insulting you at all. I just don't want you to feel like I'm pressuring you to do some shit you don't want to do. As a matter of fact, go ahead and just sit here, we'll be back. Z, its time," Dynastii said, climbing out the molester looking van with two guns at her side.

"Z I didn't mean it like I wasn't riding for y'all—" Serenity began to explain before I cut her off.

"Serenity, that's exactly what it feels like. It's cool though," I said, grabbing my gun and making sure my knives were on me. Hopping out of the van I looked around the seemingly empty block and a wicked grin spread across my face.

"The fuck are you smiling for?" Dynastii asked as I rolled up on her looking in a side window.

"You know how I feel anytime I'm about to get into some shit." I smirked. "This shit is almost better than the nut I busted earlier. So, what are we doing, going in this window or the back door?" I asked, peering in. The house was laid. I admired that the trap houses never looked like the typical ones. One would assume this was a regular ass single family home.

"Nah, I ain't never been a come in through the back-door person. I'm more of a front door type of bitch," she said, sliding both of her guns in the small of her back. I had to laugh at Dynastii. No matter how hood she wanted to act, leaving the game had made my sister a tad bit bougie. Although her ass was supposed to be dressed for a mission she was rocking a pair of distressed jeans that left damn near her whole left thigh exposed down to her knee, a crop top that said killer across it and a pair of Jordan's that looked like this was the first time they had left the box. I followed her up the front porch and waited as she knocked on the door. The sound of multiple locks could be heard and then the door swung open.

"Dynastii, what are you doing here?"

"Hey Heat, I didn't get to speak to you the other day before Polo kicked you out," she said, smiling at one of Prez's best friend.

"I was pissed you got to that nigga before I did. I was just waiting on him to grab all the re-up money. Speaking of which—" he said, looking uneasy.

"That's what I'm here for, can we discuss this inside?" she said, causing him to look uncomfortable.

"Dynastii, ma, you know you can't just walk in while I'm working," he answered, sounding unsure.

"Look, too much shit has been going on lately. I feel like I'm losing my shit so I'm going down to the Dominican Republic for a couple months. I just need to breathe. I'm catching a flight tonight so we'll have to talk when I get back," she said, wiping a stray tear. I almost applauded her ass; she deserved an Oscar Award.

"I can't wait that long Dynastii, I have to re-up ASAP. The meeting is tonight," he said, looking up and down the street. I watched as his eyes stayed on the van a minute too long and fingered the blade that I had I the front pocket of my hoodie t-shirt. "Alright y'all come in right quick," he said, walking in the house and leaving the door opened for us.

"You and Prez really go all out decorating these houses, huh?" she smiled, looking at the décor.

"Shit, if the pigs come snooping we don't want them to automatically know what's going on here. So, does Prez know you dipping on him?" he asked, staring her down.

"Heat, I'm not dipping on him. I just need to breathe for a second," she said, smoothing out her hair that was pulled into a high ponytail.

"But does he know? The Dynastii I knew would never leave that nigga's side, especially when he facing a murder charge!" he spat, shaking his head.

"Yeah well the Dynastii you knew didn't get a piece of her child delivered to her doorstep. Heat, I understand your loyalty lies with him. But I'm begging you, I need to know who Prez has beef with. Someone knows what happened to my baby." Looking at Dynastii I could tell this wasn't part of the plan. She was acting out on emotion at this point.

"You gotta talk to your man about that baby girl, that ain't my business. My main concern is the money at this point," He said. I watched as Dynastii nodded her head before pulling out her matching Glocks. She loved those damn guns and her extra ass had the nerve to get them customized in the Tiffany and Companies' signature blue. "What the fuck, you pulling out on me Dynastii?" He roared.

"Nothing personal, but our concern is the money," I said before walking up behind him and knocking him upside the head with my Beretta. As his body fell to the ground I looked at Serenity and saw the anger in her eyes.

"You good, ma?" I asked her.

"All these niggas we done ran on today and none of them are talking, Z. I want to know who the fuck had the balls to fuck with me and mine," she said. "Let's drag his big ass out of here," she said but as soon as we touched his body gunshots erupted from outside. Both pulling our guns, we eased up towards the door before it swung open.

"Take one more fucking step and taking yo shit clean off your shoulders." Dynastii spat before Serenity came into view. "What the fuck was all that shooting?" Dynastii asked not lowering her guns.

"That nigga must have known something was up and called backup. Two niggas was looking around the house so I pushed their shit back. We gotta bounce," she said. "I pulled the van in front let's, get him to the spot. That meeting going be starting real soon." Thirty minutes later we were pulling up to an old abandoned building with a now alert, tied up Heat.

"Dynastii, you on some fuck shit right now," he said, grilling Dy and refusing to enter the building.

"Nah nigga, what were your words again, the money is your only concern, well it's mine too. Stop playing with me and walk in that building before I knock your dumb ass out and roll you in the building!" she spat. He knew she was playing no games because he damn near ran into the building and walked until his eyes fell on the other men.

"What the fuck, so y'all just on a killing spree or some shit?" Heat asked, looking at the group of men in a cage.

"Shit, they ain't dead, I knocked them out. Like this," I said as I tied the chloroform soaked bandana across his face. Good thing his arms were tied up because he was trying his hardest to shake the bandana from his face.

"I meant to ask you earlier, why have you been tying it? In the movies, they sniff it for a second and then they're good," Serenity asked.

"Don't believe everything you see on television. You have to inhale it for at least five minutes. Plus, I tie theirs on a little longer so they don't wake anytime soon," I said as I watched Heat's movement slow until he fell asleep.

"Thank you for coming through," Dynastii finally said to Serenity. "You most likely saved our lives," she mumbled.

"Dynastii, I wasn't going to leave y'all hanging man. I'm just a lil' worried. Sage may joke and clown but shit him and Tec are no joke. Hell, we all did the research. We know these niggas don't care about dropping bodies. Fuck Tec used to be a menace. You were something serious way back when Dy, but even your reputation doesn't match up to his," Serenity finally voiced her concerns.

"So what you think I'm supposed to do? Walk away. For me that shit ain't an option," Dynastii said, motioning for one of our workers to drag Heat into the cage. She was quiet for a moment before she spoke again. "Check it, I'm not asking y'all to do nothing y'all don't want to. That goes for you too, Z. I am probably being hella reckless. That nigga could take this as a slap to the face and decide to kill me. Or I can earn my respect and he put me on. Either way it goes, I'm going through with my plan. The difference between y'all and me is I have nothing to live for anymore. I'm going all in because it could either lead me to my son's killer or lead me to being with him once again. This is up to y'all," she finished, walking out the building.

"You do what you want, but I ride for my family," I said, following my sister out. I was big on loyalty and I would never give anyone reason to question mine. I was riding for someone who never hesitated to ride for me.

Chapter 6:

Dynastii

"Ok, so how we are doing this tonight?" Serenity asked, walking up alongside Mizanii and I. I looked at her and chuckled before pulling her into a hug. It's not that I didn't think she had it in her, it's just I had no room for uncertainty. One moment's hesitation is all it takes for someone to end my life, and I take my shit seriously.

"I don't know about y'all but I'm hungry. I'll go home whip something up and get ready. You coming home now, Z?" I asked as we watched a few of the men burn the van we used.

"Nah, I'm going ride with Serenity," Z answered. "We'll be there before the meeting to get ready at the house though."

"Alright see you at around seven," I answered as we all went our separate ways. Heading home, I saw that I had a few missed calls and knew exactly who they came from. As if he knew I was thinking of him my phone beeped letting me know he was facetiming me. I checked my reflection in my visor and answered the call with my eyes focused on the road.

"Damn, where you been?" he asked without as much as a hello.

"Why hello to you too, President. I'm doing perfectly fine and yourself?" I said with sarcasm dripping from my tone. Briefly taking my eyes off the road, I looked down and saw the pissed off look he was flashing my way.

"Dynastii, stop playing with me. Why every time I call your ass lately I can never get through to you? And when you finally call back your ass always in a car? Where are you leaving from?" Looking over my shoulder, I pulled over to the side of the road to let this nigga know what it was.

"Prez, what are you trying to accuse me of? You know I hate when a motherfucker beats around the bush."

"Shit, I feel like you fucking around since a nigga's on lock. If you are that's fucked up! As soon as a nigga is down and out, you show your ass. Do you not realize who held you down all these fucking years?" he said, causing me to bite my cheeks to stop the tears from falling. Just that quick he had pissed me off.

"This is my last time telling you, don't ever question where I stand with your ass. Nigga, I held yo bitch ass down when you had me in these streets looking stupid. Nigga, every time you did me grimy, I held shit down. Before you open your mouth to question my loyalty check your motherfucking self. And if I do decide to step out charge it to my heart and not my pussy, nigga maybe I'm playing get back! Fuck off my phone, nigga!" I spat before disconnecting the call and blocking his number. This nigga had me fucked up. I drove home in a daze; I couldn't tell you how I safely made it there. Climbing in the bed, I pulled my son's teddy bears towards me and inhaled his scent until I dozed off.

"Dy, wake up ma," Serenity said, shaking me from my sleep.

"What time is it?" I asked

"A lil' after seven. Get dressed we need to be there before he figures out they ain't showing up," she said, causing me to jump up and head to the shower. Washing my bundles, I let them curl up in its natural body wave texture before I focused on my body. My mind drifted to Prez. Lord knows I loved that man deep in my soul, but I was starting to feel like we had been through too much. I was seeing him in a different light. For once, I didn't view him as my protector. He failed me and he failed our family. Our relationship was in the balance but the type of woman I am wouldn't allow me to leave when he needed me the most. The water running cold let me know I had been in this tub way too long. Drying off, I walked into my room and into my small closet. I knew I would never be able to live in the house Prez purchased for us again, but I didn't want to overstay my welcome at Mizanii's place either. I would be looking for a spot no later than next week.

The urge to look a lil' fancy for the meeting crossed my mind so I did just that. I grabbed a black leather wrap skirt with gold studs, a white blouse that did this lil' criss-cross across my breast and a pair of gold and black peep toe heels and placed it on the bed. I said a prayer as I applied lotion to my body. I was still so pissed from the conversation I had with Prez earlier and I didn't want to walk into this meeting with those emotions. I needed a clear head so that's what I prayed for. After applying light makeup and a red lipstick, I was ready to slide on my clothing.

"Well damn, are you sure we going handle business?" Mizanii asked, walking into the room as I slid on my last heel.

"Yeah why do you ask?" I asked, standing to my feet.

"Well, shit cause you look like you going on a date. Don't get me wrong, you look bomb but bitch can you run in those heels if shit go left?"

"Probably not but if shit goes left I ain't running anyway. I'm shooting until shit goes right," I said, grabbing both of my guns. I tucked one in the small of my back and threw the other in my gold clutch.

"Let me find out you trying to impress Tec though." She smirked.

"Umm, your ass is not looking too shabby either," I replied, looking over her attire, some black leather tights, a fitted midriff top and a pair of ankle boots. I laughed as she spun around showing out.

"I mean who said I have to dress like a nigga to play their game?" she asked as Serenity walked in and started modeling her fitted red jumpsuit and some black thigh high boots that laced up.

"Yaaaasssss bitch!" I said as she twerked in the middle of the floor. "No but for real, let's run through this. I feel like after tonight we will have the connect that we need to really make some noise in these streets. I'm freezing everyone out until I get some fucking answers. Once I dry up the streets, they goin' talk or starve. Whichever they pick is alright with me."

"So after you get your answers then what? Are we walking away from the streets?" Mizanii asked a question I didn't have the answers to just yet.

"To be real Z, I haven't thought that far. I literally have tunnel vision at the moment. My main goal is to find my son's killer. I don't even know what I'm going to do when I find out who they are. All I know is they goin' regret disrespecting me, and if I'm not satisfied then their family has to feel my pain too," I answered truthfully. Looking at my watch, I saw it was time to head over to their meet-up spot. "It's time to do this ladies," I said, walking out the room with them following behind me. After locking up the house, we were speeding off to the meeting that wouldn't be happening.

"So are we sitting in the car or we going in?" Mizanii asked as we sat in the lot with only two other cars.

"Nah, I'm going sit on his truck. They'll be coming out soon," I said, stepping out of the car and hopping on the hood of the Ford truck, trying my best not to scratch it with my heels.

"How the fuck you know this one is his?" Serenity asked sitting on top of the other car.

"Shit, because Sage ass is the flashy one. This nigga real life got a metallic gold Aston Martin, son. This truck is more so Amir's lane," I said, leaning against his window and crossing my legs.

"Y'all asking to get shot, huh? Bitch, I would shoot y'all if I walked out to you bitches on my ride," Mizanii said, walking up and passing me a blunt.

"Z, do me a favor and pull on Sage's door please. I don't have the patience for them to realize their people ain't coming," I said, inhaling and exhaling some bomb ass weed. Seconds later the alarm and lights of the flashy ass car caused them to run out the house with guns drawn.

"Man, what the fuck?" Amir said, walking over to me with an evil glare on his face. "How the fuck y'all know where this warehouse was?" Instead of answering him, I blew the weed in his face.

"Niggas are so rude these days," I said, looking at Mizanii and Serenity who were leaning against the Aston Martin laughing. "This is the second person who said fuck a greeting and just snapped on a bitch," I said before looking at a pissed off Amir. "Hello Amir, my day has been wonderful and yours?" I smiled.

"I'm not with all the games, baby girl. How you find my spot?" he asked still mugging me. Turning to the side of the truck I gracefully jumped down, fixed my skirt, and then made my way in front of him. "Let's stop fucking around and tell me what's good," he said, pulling at his beard.

"Let's. I came to you with cash on hand and offered to put more money in your pockets. You shot me done for no reason other than I was a female. I guess you felt like I couldn't hold any weight in a man's game, right?" I paused as he nodded his head at my question. "Cool, so I decided to show you I could run circles around your niggas." Pulling out my iPhone, I dialed a number and waited as they answered the facetime call. Turning my phone towards Amir I smiled as his eyes bulged at the sight before him. One of my men had the camera trained on every man on Amir's payroll in this area. I hung up the phone then smiled at him. "Let me explain something real quick. Men love saying this is a man's game but women could help y'all easily overcome obstacles in this game. Y'all act on impulse and we think things through until the end. Y'all play checkers and we play chess. Checkmate baby boy." I smiled as I blew him a kiss.

"You sure you don't want to marry me, man?" Sage asked, interrupting the intense stare down Amir and I had going on. "Like if you marry me I can be like the house husband and shit. *I'll buy your clothes; I'll cook your dinner too. Soon as I get home from work.*" He started singing causing me to laugh because he actually did sound good.

"Sage, bruh—" Amir started but Sage sung louder.

"*I'll pay your rent, Your faithful lover. Soon as I get home, soon as I get home from work.*" He sang until we were all laughing except Amir. "Man Tec, yo ass stay blocking," he said, mugging Amir.

"Now where were we, oh yeah, I remember," I said, smiling. "So the first rejection was because this was a man's game, I proved it wasn't. The second was your roster was full, right?" I asked for the confirmation I knew would come. Slowly he nodded his head. "Right, you have room now actually. I can't work with weak men and Greg told me where your spot was way too easily. So, I canceled that ass like Nino," I said with a huge grin on my face. "This is the part where you tell me thank you." To my surprise, he chuckled and nodded his head as he stroked his beard. Why did that man bite his bottom lip while openly checking me out, Lord? The floodgates opened and I was glad I wore panties under this skirt.

"Okay, we can discuss y'all joining the team," he said, causing me to smile. Walking towards the doors of the warehouse, he stopped me in my tracks. "Nah shawty, not tonight."

"I don't see why we should procrastinate but okay. How about the same time tomorrow?" I threw out there.

"Yeah that's good," he answered.

"Cool, I'll see you here tomorrow?" I said, switching directions and walking to my car.

"Wrong, *you and I* will meet elsewhere," he said, putting emphasis on the you and I. "I'll text you the reservations," he said, causing me to stare at him for a second.

"Umm, n- no. I don't think that's a good idea. I'm in a relationship so I don't do private dinner meetings," I answered, twisting my ring around my finger.

"This ain't a dinner meeting ma, we're going on a date. And leave that fucking ring home or I'm leaving."

"And if I decline?" I questioned.

"Then the offer is off of the table. Wear something sexy too," he said, hopping in his truck and pulling off before I could say anything. I'm glad he did because I didn't have the power to turn him down. I actually wanted to be on that date. And if he wanted sexy then fuck it he got that.

Chapter 7:

Tec

"Damn," I found myself saying aloud as Dynastii walked in the room commanding the attention of every man in the building. Whether they were alone, with a colleague, a wife, a girlfriend, or a mistress their eyes followed her until she stood in front of me; and even after I pulled out her chair and she took her seat.

"Sexy enough?" she smirked.

I let my eyes roam on the fitted white dress she was wearing. Dynastii looked like she had just left from an art gallery where the main attraction was her and the dress that she wore was so fitted to her curves it had to be painted on. My eyes dropped to the white heels she wore that had these elaborate gold wings on them.

"Hell yeah," I honestly answered as a smile spread across her face. "I ordered for you since you said you would be a lil' late and had never been here. I hope that's fine with you?" I threw that information out there as a test. I wanted Dynastii in the worse way but what I wouldn't deal with is a female that thought her balls hung lower than mine. My woman needed to let me be the man. It's enough her ass was trying to be in the traps and shit. I had an assumption that her getting in the game had something to do with her child's death. I needed to make sure of that. If that were the case, I would happily handle her beef because I didn't want my woman in the streets if she didn't need to be.

"That's fine, actually thank you for that. I hope you didn't order me a salad though because you'll be eating that and I'm eating what you ordered. As you can see, I'm not a salad type of girl." She laughed as the waitress came over with our drinks. "Thank you," she said with a smile.

"So Dynastii, what's your story?" I asked.

"Oh, we're about to do this?" she smiled.

"What exactly do you mean by do this?" I questioned.

"Acting as if this is an actual date."

"It is an actual date, what you mean. We are at this fancy ass restaurant, you wore that nice ass dress and I'm looking fly as shit. Don't lie you see me." I joked as she rolled her eyes. "You goin' act like you don't want to give me the pussy at the end of the night and like the perfect gentleman I won't pressure you," I finished as she started laughing. Her laugh was contagious. It wasn't over the top and loud, yet it wasn't too soft and annoying. It was strong but feminine. I couldn't help but to join her in the laughter.

"Whatever you say Amir. I don't really have a story, I'm just... regular." she said as she shrugged.

"Regular? Nah ma, extraordinary, tantalizing, exquisite, vivacious, rare. Those words describe you, don't ever call yourself regular. You far from that, I promise you." I watched as she blushed.

"Amiiirrr, I don't know what you want me to say. You start first, you putting me on the spot." She giggled.

"Ok. My aunt B raised me, that lady is my heart and then some. I have an annoying little sister named Amor. She as spoiled as they come and I am to blame for that. My other brother, Ahmad, was killed. We still don't know by who but I know the why. It's only a matter of time until I find the person responsible. Anyway, I was born and raised here and this will forever be home. I have no hidden kids and no hidden women. Now I'm what you call a regular nigga. I don't have a nine to five because I work until I can't work anymore. I buy houses, fix them up, and sell them for in most cases triple what I paid for them. The street shit ain't what I chose to do. I'm the perfect example of the game choosing me. That's about it. Your turn."

"Well, you know my sisters Mizanii and Serenity. Although, Mizanii and I came from the same female, Serenity is as close to blood as it gets. I never met my daddy but my mama decided that raising kids wasn't her niche. We received a check every month though until we turned eighteen so she can't be bad off. Prez damn near raised me; he and his mama taught me how to be a woman. Then I taught Mizanii. Serenity's story is for her to tell so I won't touch on that. You know my relationship status so I won't touch on that either. I have no job; all I know is hustle," she said, dropping her head in embarrassment as our food arrived. I nodded at the waitress before grabbing her chin.

"Don't ever put your head down, you're a queen. Hold that shit up. All you know is survival and I can respect the fuck out of that, ma," I said before cutting my steak into strips. I decided to get myself a steak, twice-baked potato and broccoli. Dynastii had some type of pasta that I had to try. Grabbing a clean forked, I reached across the table only for her to quickly hit my fork with hers.

"You can slide that hand across this table if you want to but I guarantee you will pull back a nub." She laughed popping a fork full of pasta in her mouth and moaning seductively. I don't know if it was purposely done but shorty made me instantly brick.

"Dynastii, I really can't get none of that pasta?" I asked dead ass serious. That shit was calling my name.

"You sharing a piece of your steak?" her greedy ass asked, causing me to laugh.

"Yeah bruh. Here," I said, faking an attitude as I held out my fork.

"Nah Amir, slide some of those potatoes on that fork too. You being stingy with the meat." She laughed.

"Shit, I ain't stingy with the meat at all. You want some?" I said arching my eyebrows. She chuckled at my double meaning and wrapped her lips around my fork. This time the groaning came from my mouth. In the same fashion, she offered me some pasta and that shit was rolling. "Damn!" I said chewing on what I knew was lobster.

"Right, it's bomb as shit," she said, scooping up another fork full. "And you ain't getting anymore." She laughed as she pointed her fork at me.

"So, why the streets? What makes you want to get in this grimy business?" I stopped beating around the bush and asked.

"Money," she answered.

"Your pockets ain't hurting, try again," I called her out. I know I was a nigga but like I said I had a spoiled lil' sister, I knew Dynastii's fit tonight excluding the bag was more than most people's monthly income.

"You can never have too much money, Amir," she said, avoiding my gaze.

"Dynastii, don't insult me, ma. You can't even look me in the eye. Give me the truth," I pressed.

"I need answers on what happened to my son. Someone had to have beef with Prez for them to violate in such a manner. I'm going take over then freeze the lil' niggas out. If I put them in a life or death situation like, starvation, their ass goin' sing like Jennifer Hudson," she replied, staring me down with fire and tears in her eyes.

"Tell me about your son?" I asked to calm her back down. I watched joy feel her eyes and a subtle smile grace her face.

"Malakhi was my life in the short amount of time I was blessed with him. He was bubbly and the most handsome little boy ever. With a head full of hair and long lashes, he looked like a little girl. He was sooooo beautiful; I used to stare at him sleep for hours. He never cried, not even when the doctor popped him. Now that I think about it, he just kind of chuckled. He was my why to get through life. When I had him, I gave up the running in the streets. I started going to school and had even gotten my GED. The plan was to attain a bachelor's degree but then everything happened. And the thought of school just kind of faded away." She shrugged it off and wiped a single tear from her eye.

"Don't do that. Don't act like school means nothing to you. Your eyes shined so bright when you spoke of Malakhi and school. That shit matters to you. What did what's his face say about you dropping out?" I asked like I didn't know that lil' nigga name. I knew exactly who Prez was. He was some lil' nigga trying to play in a big man's game. I watched as she angrily chuckled.

"That nigga told me school isn't for everyone. He hated that I was trying to better myself and never let me live down that he wanted the old Dynastii back," she said, pissing me off.

"What type of nigga says that type of shit? I would never want my woman in these streets. Don't get me wrong I've ran into my fair share of boss bitches, but the game turned their asses cold. I don't want that for you. Let's make a deal." I offered.

"Ok, what is it?" she asked giving me her undivided attention.

"You enroll back into school and say fuck this street shit. Let me handle the tracking down of Prez's beef. I mean I have more connections than you anyway, it'll be easier."

"What, no I can't do th—." she started before I cut her off.

"Listen, you don't know me enough to trust me so I won't say trust me. But believe in a nigga enough to know I make shit happen. Go back to school and continue making your son proud. I got you. My word is all I got and I'm giving you that," I said before she started laughing.

"Your ass is sitting on millions I'm sure, talking about your word is all you got," she said as I joined in on her laughter.

"I mean a nigga got a lil' more than his word but it's the most valuable." I laughed. "Ma, I saw how sad you got when you said hustling is all you know, we can change that. Shit, go to school to be a real estate agent, then you can help me sell these homes," I suggested, causing her to smile.

"Ok, I'll attempt to fall back. I don't know if that's really possible, but I'll try," she promised.

"That's all I ask. You can give me any information you already have tomorrow, after we sign you back up for school," I said just as I heard someone clearing their throat.

Chapter 8:

Ashanti

"Welcome to Aria, can I get you started with drinks?"

"Yeah, I would like a stray cat," I answered the waitress who looked like she was ready to pop from the two sizes too small button down.

"I'll have the same," my best friend Chloe said.

"Okay ladies, here is your menu. I'll be back in a second with your drinks and to take your order." She smiled and walked away.

"So how is my godchild? I feel like you never allow me to see him anymore." She said damn near causing me to roll my eyes.

"Chloe please, if you wanted to see Ezra you could. You have two vehicles and you know exactly where I stay," I said, calling her out on her bullshit.

"You know I've been so busy lately. Anyway, how are you and Amir?" she quickly changed the subject.

"Amir and I are doing great, working on our issues and what not. Ezra and I will be back home where we belong in no time," I said, flashing a reassuring smile. I know we weren't exactly one foot in the door but it would happen. Amir loved me more than he loved himself.

"So, is he allowed to see other people while y'all are on this lil' break, as you called it?" she asked, pulling me from my thoughts. I cocked my head as I looked at her, True Chloe was my best friend but you know what they say about birds of a feather.

I was as grimy as they came but she exceeded me in that department. I didn't have a problem because that didn't concern me but if she thought she was getting with Amir she could hang that shit up. "Fix your face; I don't want him I'm simply asking. I mean you are still speaking to Ezra's father, right?" She asked, setting my mind at ease.

"Yeah but that's different, Ezra's father and I are bonded for life. We share a beautiful baby boy. Plus, Amir thinks I cut all ties with him. The other day when I was there, he damn near begged me to stay. Had Sage not shown up, I would have too," I lied.

"That damn Sage knows he can get this work. I have never seen a white boy so fine. All I need is one night!" she said, gazing off into the distance. "Anyway, you haven't answered. Are y'all allowed to see other people?"

"What's it to you? Of course, he can't see other people!" I snapped as the waitress placed our drinks down.

"Do you need more time?" she asked, causing me to wave her off. Her rude ass saw we were having a conversation.

"Like I was saying, I wish the fuck my fiancé would be seeing other people," I continued as she sipped her drink.

"Damn, you should have saved that wish for a million dollars or something." She smirked.

"Huh?" I was genuinely puzzled until she pointed behind me. My heart rate sped up as I spun around and my eyes landed on Amir having what looked like a very intimate dinner with some female. I couldn't move as I sized her up. "Who is that ugly bitch?" I mumbled to myself but obviously not low enough. I watched Chloe rummage through her clutch before she handed me her prescription glasses. "What the fuck are you handing me these for?" I snapped.

"Because you obviously need these more than I do. Stop hating that girl is bad. She looks like one of those Instagram famous chicks," she said, staring the girl down.

"Damn bitch, why don't you take a fucking picture? I assure you it'll last longer!" I snapped, taking my anger out on her. "The bitch looks like some cheap thrill if you ask me," I said, throwing mad shade.

"You see that Birkin? It hasn't even hit stores yet. Those Giuseppe's she's rocking, that's twice your rent. Baby girl, is everything but cheap or ugly. Amir surely knows how to pick them." She smiled, pissing me off. It's like she was enjoying my heartbreak. Standing up I made me way to the bathroom and had a slight break down. I felt a panic attack coming so entered the stall and attempted to calm my breathing. After a few moments, I found myself walking out of the bathroom and past my table where Chloe was eating. The bitch didn't even wait on me to order her appetizer. Standing in front of their table pissed me off more because they were so into their conversation they didn't notice me standing there until I cleared my throat.

"Speak of the damn devil, Ashanti?" Amir asked like he wasn't sure it was me. I had to stop the tears from falling from my eyes. This bitch was so pretty it hurt.

"What the fuck is this, Amir?" I asked, crossing my arms across my chest. I watched his eyes fall on her then look back my way.

"This is a nice restaurant that you're causing a scene at," he smartly replied.

"Amir, don't test me because a scene will be the least of your worries. I will fucking cause a full length paramount picture in this bitch. How dare you embarrass me like this?" I said, lowering my voice a little. Looking over at my table, I saw Chloe sipping on her drink while her eyes were trained on us. That fucking bitch was enjoying this.

"How am I embarrassing you, Ashanti? Take your ass home!" he said, thinking he would dismiss me.

"Do you know that he is engaged?" I asked staring a hole into the side of her head. I was pissed off because she looked unbothered with me sitting here. When she ignored my question, I snapped my fingers in her face but I quickly regretted that decision. I felt my finger crack as she squeezed my hand and pulled me closer to her.

"I'm a grown ass woman, not your child. You want to snap at someone, then snap at his ass. Make that your last time disrespecting me, k?"

When she released my hand, she shoved me causing me to bump into the table immediately behind me. "Amir, handle your business love. Give me a call later and we can discuss that thing." She winked before grabbing her bag and strolling out the restaurant as if she owned the bitch. It pissed me off that even my eyes stayed on her until I could no longer see her. I looked at Amir waiting on an explanation I never got. He threw a few bills on the table and stood to leave.

"Amir, you owe me an explanation," I said once I followed him out. He had already had his truck door open as I stood a few feet away. Slamming the door, he walked towards me causing me to flinch.

"Bitch, I don't owe you shit. That was unfucking called for! Newsflash Ashanti, we ain't together and we not getting back together, EVER. Move the fuck on. You can't afford to be in this bitch eating out anyway! Your bills about to be due and this bank is fucking closed." He mugged me and hopped in his truck. Without another look my way, he pulled off.

The tears fell as I walked to my car and sped out of the parking lot. I wasn't crying because I was in love with Amir. I was crying because his income is something I didn't want to lose. I had a fear of being broke; I wouldn't go back to penny, nickel, diming. I couldn't believe I was losing Amir!

I know I fucked up having another man's baby but like I said, that nigga loved my dirty things. When he started accepting Ezra, I thought we could make shit work. I knew my baby father wouldn't let me live happily ever after with him but in the mean time I would enjoy the perks. Amir was fucking paid. Although he tried to hide it, I knew what I knew. His brother Ahmad had more money than a lil' bit and when he was killed that all became Amir's. He was basically handed over the keys to the streets and what did he do? Hand, it over to Sage. I wouldn't have a problem with him doing that if I could finesse Sage, but his ass was loyal and genuinely hated my guts. The ringing of my phone caused me to look down at the screen. I quickly ignored Chloe's call; fuck her. When she called again I answered with as much attitude as I could muster.

"What the fuck do you want?" I screamed into the phone.

"Bitch, who are you talking to?" my baby's father asked.

"Oh, I'm sorry baby, I thought you were Chloe. I've been waiting on your call Prez." The reason I couldn't love Amir is because I was in love with another woman's man. I knew he was taken when I met him almost two years ago but I didn't care. I wanted him and I always get what I want.

"Are you in the car? The fuck you coming from this late?" he questioned, causing me to roll my eyes. He was so fucking controlling.

"Dinner with Chloe. Tec was there with some bitch," I said before I thought about what I was saying.

"You sound mad. What the fuck that gotta do with you?" he snapped.

"I mean, nothing. I was just saying," I mumbled.

"Get fucked up if you want to. Come see me tomorrow," he demanded as usual. Prez never asked me for things, he demanded.

"Ok. I'll bring Ezra to see you too," I said smiling.

"You do what you want with that lil' nigga," he said before

hanging up in my ear. I hated that Prez refused to bond with our son. I know it was because he didn't want his other bitch to know about him. I was already planning of getting rid of that hoe before Prez came home. I was ready to have the family I deserved.

Chapter 9:

Dynastii

"So how was the date?" Mizanii asked as she and Serenity lay across my bed.

"It wasn't a date Z, it was a business dinner," I corrected.

"Girl, did you see what you wore, baby that was a date. And if you would have stayed out late I would have thought it was a nasty date," Serenity said, laughing.

"Yep, the nastiest! Bih you went get your snatch waxed!" Mizanii laughed.

"Mind y'all damn business, get out my damn room." I joined in on the laughter.

"Uh, uh, this my house boo," Mizanii said. "I don't even know why you going visit Prez ass. Y'all haven't spoken since the falling out."

"Yeah that's why I'm going there. I need to know exactly what's going on with us. I won't leave him high and dry but if I'm single then let me know that," I said, slipping on some light wash jeans a pink V-neck and some pink and grey Nikes.

In my mind, I was still trying to form the words I would say to Prez but they wouldn't come. After making sure I had everything in order, I said my goodbyes and was on my way to the prison. I don't know why I was so nervous but I couldn't get my legs to stop shaking if I tried as I sat in the private visiting room waiting on Prez.

"Dynastii?" he asked, looking shocked. I charged it to the fact that we weren't on speaking terms.

"Don't look so surprised; who else would it be silly," I said, standing to my feet and offering a hug that he returned.

"Well I mean I wasn't expecting you. You look good. I like the new hair on ya. It reminds me of the old Dy." He smiled. "Speaking of which, I spoke with Heat," he said, causing me to roll my eyes. After I set up the dinner date with Amir I had my people clear out the warehouse and leave that cage open. When the men woke up, all of their cars were waiting for them.

"Ok. And?" I questioned.

"Dynastii what the fuck you think you doing son? I can't protect your ass from in here! You're playing a dangerous game!" he said, hitting the table in front of me.

"Nigga and until I get answers I'll play this game with the settings on hard! I'm all Malakhi has! I'm the only person going hard for him. Fuck you mean you can't protect me. Do I look like I need protecting? Worry about protecting Heat. They the ones got caught slipping!" I spat as angry tears fell from my eyes.

"Oh, so you don't need a nigga, Dynastii? The fuck you mean you the only one looking out for Malakhi?" he said nervously looking around me. "Look I ain't in the right headspace to argue with you today. You can go; we'll talk some other day," he said, shocking me.

"Nigga, are you dismissing me? I drove all this way and you think I'm just goin' leave like that?" I asked.

"Yep. I ain't got time to argue with you Dynastii. Every time you come up here, it seems like yo ass bring nothing but drama. I told you I can't deal with this shit while I'm behind bars!" he snapped.

"Nigga, it seems like you just picking an argument. You brought this shit up not me. Look maybe it is best that I go," I said, standing to my feet half expecting him to stop me.

"Yeah you right, you should go. Guards!" he screamed just as the guard walked in with someone following behind him. I knew it was a female by the heels she wore. I couldn't make out who she was because she was directly behind the guard and her face was half covered by the child she was holding.

"You have another visitor Pierre, your fiancée' and son." The guard smirked. I looked at the nervous expression on Prez's face and knew my world had been flipped upside down.

"I don't have no fiancée man," was all Prez offered. Before I could say anything, my eyes landed on the woman that stepped into view. The smile on her face almost sent me to jail, because I wanted to tap her ass in here, cops and all.

"You fucking my fiancé and I'm fucking yours. Checkmate hoe," Ashanti smirked.

"Who the fuck you fucking, Dynastii?" Prez had the nerve to question. Chuckling I wiped the single tear that escaped my eye.

"You wasn't worried about Malakhi because you had a replacement, huh. That's a wrap for us President. I can't and won't compete with a baby," I said, getting up and walking out of the door on the other side of the room.

I didn't trust myself to pass near her or her child. Besides looking that child in the face would make this shit too real. Once I was hidden behind the tint of my car, I finally broke down. How the fuck could he do this to me? A baby though? I sat in that parking lot for what felt like hours until I was able to pull myself together and leave.

"Hello?" I answered my ringing phone without looking at the screen.

"Um, did I catch you at a bad time?" I heard Amir's voice.

"If this is about business then no. There's never a bad time. Wassup?" I asked, trying to clear my voice.

"Ok. Perfect then I'll text you an address, meet me here." He said before disconnecting the call. Seconds later, he sent over an address, which I forwarded to my sister so she could know where I was.

I drove until I pulled up to the most beautiful home I'd ever seen. It wasn't huge, but it was definitely big enough. I parked behind Amir's truck and he came around to open the door in just a pair of jeans and some construction boots.

"Umm interesting get up. Are you just coming home from work?" I asked.

"No, I'm still at work, this is what I do," he said, motioning towards the house behind me. "I told you, I buy old houses and fix them up then sell them," he cleared that up.

"This house doesn't look old, I love it," I said, looking towards the house once again.

"That's because you see the finished product. I have some pictures inside of what it looked like before. Come in," he said, leading me towards the paved walkway and up the front steps. The porch on the house was huge and I could imagine just sitting here in the evenings.

"The owners won't care that you're letting me in here?" I asked as he opened the front door.

"The house isn't on the market yet. I have a lil' more work to do then Sage has to come run a few wires," I heard him talking but I really wasn't paying attention. I was too focused on the open layout of the house. I fell in love with it instantly. "Here is what it looked like when I got it," he said, showing me pictures of the house.

"Wow it doesn't even look like the same house. You're amazing at what you do. So again, why are you in the streets, I can imagine this is good money."

"I told you some things you can't escape. Your ass wasn't trying to jump head first in the streets because you wanted to. The other night when we talked you were so excited about school. Your eyes lit up when you talked about your goals. We are both victims of our circumstances," he said, staring into my eyes. Clearing my throat, I rubbed my hand against my hair and looked back at the living area.

"How many bedrooms?" I asked, changing the subject. Amir peered at me for a moment before chuckling.

"Three and a library that can double as an office," he answered.

"Bathrooms?"

"Two and a half," he answered again.

"When will you be done with this place?" I asked as I walked to the back of the house where the bedrooms were.

"About a week. Why are you asking?"

"Because I want it! I don't even care the price, I want it!" I said, spinning around to realize that he was standing too damn close for comfort.

"Well shit I want you; I don't even care the price. I want you," he said before pulling me in to him by my waist and pressing his lips against mine.

I wanted to pull away but everything in my soul felt like he needed this. It felt right being in his arms, as if nothing else mattered. Wrapping my arms around his neck, I accepted his tongue as he parted my lips. This man's tongue caressed mine and made me feel things that a kiss was never supposed to make a grown woman feel. His kiss alone was orgasmic. I have no idea if it was the fact that I hadn't had a man touch me so sensually in months or if he was that good but my legs started shaking.

"Amir, don't look at me like that," I whined after her broke the kiss. He looked at me with lust-filled eyes as he bit his bottom lip and pulled at his beard.

"Ma, I can't explain this attraction I have to you but I need you in my life. I want to wake up to you and go to sleep on side of you daily. I ain't never been the type of nigga to hid my emotions. You got me fucked up in the head," he expressed and I saw the truth starring back at me. He was laying it all on the line for me. The ball was in my court. So I either needed to shoot or pass. There was an awkward silence as we had an intense staring match before I interrupted it.

"I'm sorry," I said as I power walked towards the door and down the front steps. I was already at my car before I heard him.

"Dynastii!" he called out with so much authority in his voice I jumped. Turning around I faced him and saw the determined look on his face. "Don't do that ma, don't run from me. We're both grown, let me know what's good with you," he said, walking over to his truck and sitting in the bed of it. Closing my door, I walked over to him.

"What do you want me to say, Tec?"

'Don't start that shit; I'm never Tec to you! Tell me what you feel ma, but I want the truth uncut and unfiltered. Don't mention that nigga either because you ain't slid that ring back on your finger since I made you take it off at dinner," he said, causing me to look at my bare hands.

"It just slipped my mind," I mumbled, running my hands in my hair again. "I'm not supposed to want you, Amir. I'm not supposed to have these feelings for you. I'm not supposed to fall asleep wondering how your day was. I'm not supposed to wake up needing to hear your voice. I'm not supposed to pray for you before I pray for the nigga I supposedly love. I'm not supposed to want you to want me but I do. And I can't help it. I just broke up with my man of six years and I don't care. I know if I went home, I would still be consumed with thoughts of you. I wouldn't even care about what he had going on," I finished looking over at the wooded area. I loved the privacy that this house had, there wasn't a neighbor around, just trees.

"Dynastii, I want you. In every meaning of the word, I need you," he said, walking over to me and grabbing my face again. He kissed me with so much passion I began to wonder if I had ever been kissed properly. My body began shaking and I embarrassingly pulled away. "What's wrong?" he questioned, looking confused.

"I'm not sure but I think you made me cum from a kiss," I whispered out of breath. I watched a grin stretch across his face.

"You think, let me check." And before I could respond he lifted me from the ground and laid me out on the back of his truck.

"Ammiiirrrrr," I said.

"Shhh, I'm just checking," he answered as he pulled my jeans and panties completely off and placed them on the truck besides me. Seconds later, I tensed up as he spread my legs and took swiped his tongue in the folds of my pussy.

"Ssssss," I hissed as I sucked in a breath.

"Yeah, you may have cum but I'm sure you can do better," he said before spreading my lips, you know *those lips,* and began eating my soul through my pussy. Amir's long tongue touched places I forgot was there and some I never knew. "Stop fucking running," he said into my pussy while pulling me back down to the edge of the truck. When he slid his thick tongue into my pussy and flicked it that pushed me over the edge. I began nutting even more as I listened to the slurping noise he was making.

"Oh Amirrrrr! Fuckkkkkk!" I moaned as he continued sucking on my now sensitive clit. I was in need of some dick and was just about to tell him so until I was interrupted.

"Amor, remind me that Amir is no longer allowed to eat off of my silverware with his nasty ass."

Chapter 10:

Tec

Hearing my Aunt B's voice caused me to freeze up. I quickly grabbed Dynastii's clothing and slid her panties and jeans back on before I spin around. I had to stop myself from laughing because Dynastii was grabbing the back of my shirt as she held me,

"Hey Aunt B and Amor, what are y'all doing here?" I asked as they leaned against Dynastii's car.

"Well, we came bring you some food, but it seems like you made arrangements for lunch already. Are you full?" Amor asked, making Aunt B pop her behind the head.

"Who is your lil' lady friend ain't no use in not speaking, she was real vocal a second ago. C'mon on out here chile," she said, talking to Dynastii. Her grip tightened on my shirt so I stepped to the side so Aunt B could see her. I laughed as she looked at me like I betrayed her but forget that, she never got popped by Aunt B. She would get over it.

"Hello, my name is Dynastii. How are you?" Dynastii asked as her chocolate cheeks flushed red.

"Obviously not as good as you after that lil' show," she said, smiling at Dynastii. "My name is Betty but you can call me Aunt B. I would shake your hand or hug you but since you was just being a lil' nasty, I'll pass. Maybe next time we meet."

"Aunt B, c'mon man. Let me show y'all the inside of the house," I said, taking the attention off of Dynastii. We all started walking towards the house when Amor tapped me.

"Umm, are you sure she can walk?" she asked, looking at Dynastii still sitting on the back of the truck. I made my way back to her side.

"My damn legs still shaking, I think I'll fall if I stand up," she said with a flushed look on her face.

"I got you," I said, lifting her up and cradling her like a baby as I carried her in the house.

"Amir, this is embarrassing put me down." She laughed.

"My aunt saw me slurping the juice out of yo pussy, and me carrying you is embarrassing?" I whispered in her ear causing her to giggle.

"So, you're Amir's new boo?" Amor asked as soon as we met them in the kitchen.

"No, it's not like that. Amir and I are simply friends, nothing more and nothing less," she said smiling at me. I was goin' let her rock with that answer because I needed to make sure she was done with her ex dude for good. I wasn't about to do the yo-yo thing with my heart, not even for Dynastii.

"So that's what friends are doing these days? Maybe I need me a lil' friend," Aunt B said, causing me to side eye her ass.

"Yeah get homeboy fucked up if you want too," I said, dodging the punch she threw. I never let her age fool me, Aunt B can throw down.

"You better watch your damn mouth, Amir. Watch what I do to you if you keep playing with me like I'm one of your lil' friends," she said like I was still a child.

"What are we eating?" I asked, changing the subject.

"You and Dynastii can have this, Amor and I going shopping," she said, pointing at the food.

"Speaking of which..." Amor said, making me side eye her. I already knew what her ass wanted so I dug in my wallet and handed over my black card.

"Thank you big brudda," she said, kissing my cheek and heading out to the car.

"Dynastii, it was nice meeting you honey; I hope I see you again. Just with your pants on next time." Aunt B laughed giving Dynastii a hug. "Walk me out," she told me. I already knew she wanted to talk about Dynastii and I was ready for the questions. Walking to the car, I ran and jumped in Amor's selfie and laughed as she attempted to hit me.

"Go head on girl, what nigga you sending that to?" I questioned.

"Oh brother you barking up the wrong tree, I am not worried about these niggas. Trust me," she said, hopping in the Audi I had copped her last Christmas.

"Sooo Amir, Dynastii is pretty. And most importantly, she isn't Ashanti. Thank you, Jesus!" she said, causing me to laugh. My aunt and my sister hated Ashanti with a passion. My sister was forever saying it's because she saw the fake in her, whatever that means.

"Yeah, she is pretty, and she's so left of Ashanti you don't understand." I smiled, thinking of Dynastii.

"Yeah but I saw the expression on your face when she said you two were only friends. Are you sure y'all on the same page?" she questioned, causing me to think.

"I mean yeah, Dynastii has a lil' situation she has to answer before we can move forward." I replied.

"You sure she wants to move forward?"

"Dang Aunt B, just crush my dreams." I laughed.

"No, I just don't want you prematurely planning and end up heartbroken back in bed with that lil' jezebel Ashanti," she said, causing me to laugh.

"I got it covered Auntie. Let me get back in here before this girl eats all my damn food. Don't let her flat stomach fool you, she's greedy!" I said, pulling her in for a hug and tapping the top of my sister's car. Walking in the kitchen, I shook my head as her ass sat Indian style on the island busting down a plate of food.

"Amir, tell your aunt you ain't gotta go for dinner tonight if you don't want to. I will happily take your seat. Did you know your aunt could cook like this?" she asked steady stuffing her mouth.

"Man, give me my damn food with yo greedy ass." I tried to snatch the plate from her but she moved it.

"Noooo Amir, Aunt B said this was for you and me, nigga! So share, cause I damn sure will tell on you," she said, showing me the tongue. I flicked her off then grabbed the second plate out the bag. I know this lil' ass plate wasn't going to fill me up, that's why she always packed me two plates. Unwrapping the plate, the aroma of the fried chicken and red beans and rice made my stomach start growling. I went to the ice chest and grabbed two bottles of water for Dynastii and me. All that could be heard was subtle chewing and no conversation what so ever.

"Damn, that was the best food I ever ate," Dynastii said unbuttoning her jeans.

"What we about to pick up where we left off?" I asked dead ass serious.

"Nigga no, my stomach just needed room to breathe." She laughed as she walked out of the kitchen.

"Where are you going, Dynastii?" I asked not moving because this food was too damn good.

"Look around my house a little more!" she screamed back. After I finished my plate, I looked around until I found her in the master suite.

"Are you serious about wanting this house?" I asked.

"Yeah, I told you I don't care about the price. This house

spoke to me as soon as I walked in." She nodded her head adamantly. "Can we change the tub in here? I always wanted a garden tub. And I saw the library; I can't wait to fill it," she said full of excitement.

"You read?" I asked her.

"Yep."

"What type of books you read?" I asked leaning against the bathroom sink.

"Any kind really, my taste in books is all over. Monday I'm into *Harry Potter* and *Twilight*, Tuesday you can find me cuddled up reading, *books by* Latoya Nicole like, *Gangsta's Paradise* and *Love & War.* Wednesday, I may be face deep in B. Capri's, *A Jackboy Stole my Heart.* Thursday, might read *Waiting to Exhale* and Friday I'm reading Mz. Lady P's *Thug Paradise.* Saturday and Sunday, I may be all into anything by Treasure Malian and Jahquel. Sunday is always saved for my bible and T.D. Jakes. It just depends on my mood really," she answered with a smile.

"So, you've always been a reader?" I asked genuinely curious.

"Since a child, yes. Outdoors was never my thing. I was always a reader before anything." She nodded.

"Ok what was your favorite childhood book?"

"Oh, that's not fair, there were so many. My top picks would have to be the *Amelia Bedelia* series, *Miss Nelson is Missing*, *Alexander and the Terrible, Horrible, No Good, Very Bad Day*, and the *Baby-sitters Club* series." Watching her eyes sparkle with excitement, planted an idea in my head. I would fill this library up with every book she loved and some she had never read. I would do anything to see this excitement on her face. "Why are you staring at me like a weirdo, Amir?" she asked, flicking my lip.

"Man, you're so beautiful, and the fact that you don't realize it makes that shit even more sexy," I stated honestly as I pulled her into my arms. "Dynastii, I'm not with the games, ma.

Seeing you with that smile on your face makes me want to be the reason it stays there. I want to be the nigga that puts it there every morning. I want to be the nigga that makes sure it's the last expression you have on your face every night. You have me ready to put a bullet in any nigga that threatens your happiness. I know you're in that lil' situationship but that nigga don't deserve you, ma. When you decided to be with him that was like you gave a crackhead a diamond. They don't know what they have in their hands. Let a real man show you your worth," I said laying all my cards on the table. I watched as her mouth opened and closed a few times but words never came out. I saw the tears well up in her eyes but they never fell.

"Amir, I want to be with you so bad but... I just got out of a long ass relationship a few hours ago. It wouldn't be fair to you or my heart," she said as I nodded.

"Don't worry about me, I can handle me. And your heart, don't worry about that either; I'll handle that for you. I'm not talking about today, Dynastii. Shit, I ain't talking about tomorrow either. I'll wait, we can move as slow or as fast as you want to. Just promise me you'll give me a chance when the time is right."

"I can make that promise," she said with a smile as I pressed my lips against hers.

"So that means I can get some pussy or I have to wait until we're together?" I asked, dodging the punch she threw my way.

"Whatever, you ain't getting shit until I have a title." She laughed.

"Look shorty that's on you, I'm trying to give you a title now. You're playing more games than the MLB."

"I'm not playing games with you, Amir. I just don't want to play with either of our hearts. I appreciate you for waiting until my mind is right. When the time is right, I'll be proud to let the world know who is daddy." She winked, causing me to brick up. She could think I wasn't getting no pussy if she wanted too. She shouldn't have called me daddy if that was the case. I would wait on that title, but I was about to make her change her mind about the rest of that shit.

Chapter 11:

Sage

"Ma, you gotta bounce. Let's go lil' mama, it's checkout time," I said to the female lying in my bed. "You can fake like you sleeping all your ass wants but when I slide you out my door, mattress and all then don't say shit to me," I said, walking in the bathroom. Turning on the shower, I waited a few minutes before grabbing my gun and opening the door. Shaking my head, I tiptoed over to where the dumb bitch was digging in my pants pocket. The feeling of my gun to the back of her head made her freeze up.

"Oh my god!" she shrieked. I noticed the bitch started pissing.

"Bruh, tell me that ain't piss leaking from your too damn old for that pussy on to my damn mattress!" I snapped. Aunt B would beat my ass if I tried to hit a woman but this bitch was about to get it. "Get yo pissy pussy ass up, bruh!" I said, snatching her purse up and pulling out her wallet. Opening it, I flipped through the bills and shook my head.

"Why are you in my wallet?" she had the nerves to question.

"Wasn't your ass just trying to run through mine? Shut the fuck up talking to me. As a matter of fact, stand in the corner and think about what you done." I motioned towards the corner with my gun. "Uh, uh face that motherfucker." Going back to her wallet, I noticed she was carrying more fucking money in this wallet then I was. *Since when bitches stopped believing in banks.* I made sure to pull out just enough money to cover the cost of my new king-sized mattress and threw her wallet back in her purse.

"Did you just steal my money?" she snapped. I looked her ass up and down with disgust before answering.

"Check it shawty come grab this end of the mattress where you couldn't control yourself. You helping me drag this motherfucker to the street," I said, sliding on my Gucci flip flops.

"I don't have on any clothes," she said as I threw on a shirt and walked off to turn the shower off. I took a deep breath before grabbing my keys and answering her.

"My eyes ain't broke ma, let's go."

"I ain't going outside naked!" she snapped. Lifting my gun, I repeated myself once more.

"Grab that fucking mattress." She quickly started dragging the mattress by herself. Good thing for her we were at my ducked off one-bedroom home. There were no neighbors that would see her naked. On the way out, I locked and closed the door behind us. Instead of helping, I followed her out the door and to the street where she dropped it. I laughed as she walked to front door and attempted to open it.

"The door is locked," she said, crossing her arms.

"No shit, I locked it. Here go your purse and keys, you gotta bounce, ma. I was goin' let you wash your ass and shit but you tried to steal from me." I laughed, hopping in one of my favorite toys, my jeep.

"Nigga, my man can't see me pull up to the house naked smelling like sex!" she screamed as I pulled off leaving her cursing me out. She would be ok. I was already pissed off I had to go way across town to get me another mattress.

"Dial Tec," I said to my Bluetooth system.

"What the hell you want, Sage?" Dynastii answered the phone joking as usual. They had been chilling for a while but officially dating for at least two months and I loved her for Tec.

She was the complete opposite of Ashanti ass and you could tell they were both happy.

"Shit, I want your fucking sister but she's playing games with a nigga." I laughed thinking of Mizanii mean ass. She wouldn't give me the time of day but I wasn't giving up. I had showed up to her spot on more than one occasion and her ass kept threatening me with those damn knives she played with. She's gotta know that I like my women crazy and she's perfect.

"Wouldn't you have to actually be a nigga for her to give a nigga a chance Sage the Gemini." She laughed at her own joke.

"Here you go with the race jokes, huh? And what the fuck I told you about calling me that shit, Dynastii?" I asked, laughing.

"But your name is Sage and you told me you were a Gemini," she said seriously making me laugh harder.

"Does my boy know you answering his phone and shit?"

"Umm hmm, he's right here but he hurting," she answered.

"What's wrong with him?" I asked seriously.

"Oh, he ain't physically hurt. Those feelings hurt because I tapped that ass in 2K after all the bragging he was doing." She laughed before I heard a bunch of noise and then Tec's voice.

"Sage, her ass was cheating and won't give me my fucking rematch." He answered sounding pissed. I laughed because that nigga took his record on 2K and Madden serious as a heart attack. "Anyway, nigga what you up to?" he asked.

"Maaaaan, I'm heading to the fucking furniture store, this bitch pissed me off and pissed on my motherfucking bed. She almost made me want to choke her out, but I know Aunt B ass was goin' find out. I don't know how she finds out but I swear she be knowing son."

"Yeah, she would have whipped that ass. Let me get up with you a lil' later though, Dynastii's gone give me this rematch whether she want to or not," he said, laughing as I heard her scream no the fuck she was not.

"Bet." I disconnected the call.

Pulling up to Luxury Living NYC, I parallel parked and strolled inside. I saw some fly ass furniture that I wouldn't mind copping but instead of wasting time I swaggered to the back of the stores where the mattresses were.

"Hey Sage, how are you?" asked Cheyenne, a chick I used to smash on the regular. The pussy was grade A, but her fucking mouth that made it hell to be with her. A nigga couldn't take a shit without her nagging. The killing part is she was never for me; the bitch was just a jump off. Adding to that her occupation had us jumping in and out of hoops so her colleagues wouldn't see us together. I was a grown ass man and couldn't get down with being a secret.

"Shit, you know me, everything is everything. What about you, I see you look fly as usual," I said honestly. No matter the time, date, or place anytime I ran into Cheyenne she was looking like a fucking check. She had this bad ass suit that squeezed every single curve she possessed. Cheyenne was different from any chick I had fucked with; she was a professional woman that fell for my thugged out ass. I actually met shorty when I had court one morning. I had a possession charge and she was the prosecutor on the case. One recess and a hotel room later, the case was thrown out because of missing evidence and I continued tapping that ass.

"You know how I do. Anyway, Sage you are one tough guy to get a hold of," she said, looking me over while licking her full lips.

"You know the only kind of man that's always available is a broke man. Why have you been looking for me though, a nigga's been staying out of trouble." I let her know the only reason she should be checking for me is if my name came across her desk.

"So, I can't contact you outside of business matters now, Sage? Why is that?" She asked stepping a lil' closer in my space.

"Shit, I got a ten-inch-long reason. Every fucking time I put this dick in your life you get the only child syndrome," I said, walking away from her ass and towards the mattress section.

"What's the only child syndrome, Sage?" she asked not getting the hint and following me.

"You know only children that don't know how to share shit. As soon as I slide this monster in you, all I hear is, *'this is my dick, you're my man'*. That shit makes my dick forget how to get hard for you shorty," I answered before her name was called by an older white man.

"Ms. Kline, how are you today?" he asked, holding out his hand, which she quickly shook. I chuckled as she threw on her professional voice.

"Hello Richard. Are you furniture shopping also?" she asked until his eyes looked my way then hers in confusion.

"I'm sorry, are you two together?" he questioned. I watched as her face turned red and smiled. I could blow up her spot but why? I didn't want her ass.

"Nah, shorty wouldn't know how to act if she was for me. I'm just trying to buy a mattress," I said while walking away once again.

After getting help selecting my mattress I went look for some pieces for the house that Tec and I were currently working on. Most houses we flipped were sold with the furniture and appliances included; that helped them sell for top dollar. Walking towards the sectionals my eyes landed on the baddest female ever. She was chewing on her lip as she looked between two sectionals.

"Hmm, with this one I would have to buy new lamps. But with this one the color is kind of off to me," she spoke to herself aloud.

"Just buy the new lamps ma, that fucking couch is ugly," I said, pointing to the brown and mustard colored sectional she was considering. I watched as a smile graced her face before she quickly replaced it with a look of indifference; but the excitement never left her eyes.

"Sage, are you stalking me?" she asked.

"Fuck yeah! Speaking of which I passed in front of your house the other day, about four in the morning, who the fuck car was in your driveway?" I asked dead ass serious.

"You know where I stay?" she asked looking shocked.

"Shorty, give me a week and I'll know your blood type. Why you keep playing games with me?"

"I'm not in to playing any games, Sage, I'm just not going there with you," she answered honestly. "But really, how do you know where I stay?"

"What's wrong with going there with a nigga?" I ignored her question again.

"Sage, I'm really not looking to be tied down. I'm a free spirit. I'm not trying to dodge the prank calls and I ain't beat for the stalking. I watch Lifetime, you white men are crazy. All it's going to take is for your lil' dick to keep me unsatisfied, I dodge your calls and then bam I wasn't joking when I said this pussy would ruin your life." She smirked. Shaking my head, I walked up to her and pressed her body into mine by grabbing her ass.

"Let me tell you something shorty, I never spoke a word about you being mine. If you want to fuck then we can fuck and I can kick you out like the next female. Don't let the color of my skin fool you ma, ain't shit about me small." I paused to grab her hand and place it on my dick. "Nah be that same woman who just had so much mouth, grab that motherfucker right. This ain't no lifetime dick here. It is life changing however, I'll admit to that shit. When it's all said and done you goin' beg for the dick then beg for a title," I finished, grabbing her face and pouring everything I could into a kiss. I knew I was on to something when she got weak in the knees and I had to catch her. Placing her on the same mustard colored couch, I swaggered out the door.

Chapter 12:

Mizanii

BAM! BAM! BAM!

I didn't even bother using the doorbell as I impatiently bang on the door for someone to open the door. As soon as it swung open, I started going on.

"I should shoot your ass in the pinky toe for introducing me to that slim shady ass nigga!" I told a laughing Tec. I noticed he was dressed in all black and looked like he was either just getting in or on his way out. "Tec, nothing is funny, I hate his ass!" I said as he followed me around the house looking for Dynastii.

"Hello to you too Mizanii, how are you this afternoon? I'm great, by the way," his sarcastic ass said. "What did Sage do to you now?" he asked, laughing. Walking into the master suite I saw Dynastii playing with Bella and Mafia, the two lil' ass dogs that she purchased herself so she wouldn't be lonely.

"Dynastii, can I kill Sage?" I asked as she and Tec fell out laughing.

"Over a lil' kiss?" she asked, causing me to roll my eyes.

"So he ran to y'all like a lil' bitch?" I asked.

"You was coming do the same damn thing, why won't you give my boy a chance though, Mizanii?" Tec asked, grabbing his gun and wallet. I watched as Dynastii quickly jumped up and threw on a pair of black high waisted jeggings, and a pair of Timbs. "Where the fuck are you going, Dy?" he asked, causing her to spin around.

"Don't think because Z came in here that I forgot about

that call. I'm coming with you, Amir! You said I could come along with you to any possible leads," she said, throwing a black crop top hoodie over her bra.

"Man, I don't know what the fuck this dude on, let me even see if the info he got is official. I don't want you getting your hopes up for nothing," Tec responded softening his tone.

"Tec, play with me if you want to but watch me be right back at the traps kidnapping your niggas! I'm going let your ass rock, for now," she said, mugging him.

"Who are you talking to, Dynastii? Quit playing me like I'm one of these lame ass niggas. And keep calling me Tec and watch how it happens to ya. Gimme a kiss," he said, pulling her in for a kiss. I smiled as my sister giggled. I loved Tec for her. "Alright Mizanii, stop giving my boy a hard time," he said as he wrote something on a paper and handing it to me on his way out.

"What's that?" Dynastii nosey ass asked. I read over the paper and started laughing.

"An address, most likely Sage's address. Anyway, what tip did he get?" I asked.

"Well you know he put money up for anyone who came forward with people that Prez was beefing with. This dude hit him up today and told him he had some information for him," she said sighing.

"You don't seem happy about that."

"I'm not happy about just sitting here. I know I promised Tec I would let him do him but I can't possibly focus on school-work," she stressed.

"Sit back and let that man be a man Mizanii. You have to stop being hard all the time," I said, scooping up one of her lil' fur balls. "Which one is this?" I asked.

"Bella. I know but I'm so used of handling shit on my own.

I really don't know how to play the back," she confessed.

"Yeah well that's what happens when you date a man and not a lil' pussy. I'm shocked your ass stayed put though."

"Have you met my man, Tec also known as Amir? That nigga does not play. When he says stay put, he means stay put." She laughed. "Anyway, what y'all have planned for my birthday. All his ass told me was we're getting on a plane at some point."

"Oh yeah we're going to mind yo got damn business." I laughed standing to my feet. If I stayed longer, she would surely get the secret out of me.

"That's wrong, how am I going to pack for this trip if I don't know where I'm going?" she whined.

"I'll pack for you. Goodbye and goodnight, sis," I said, throwing up the piece sign on my way out.

"Let me know you made it home safely." She screamed at my retreating back. Hopping in my car and blasted my song, DJ Luke Nasty "OTW" all the way home. I had recently decided to redecorate my home so I threw everything out until my furniture was delivered. The lack of things in my home had it feeling really cold and lonely. Nights like this I missed my sister being down the hall. It was nothing for me to go bother her.

Big Sis: I know your ass made it home already, Z.

Me: Damn I JUST walked in my house botheration.

Big Sis: So, you should have JUST let me know you were home, have me worrying about your ass.

Me: Well you can stop worrying because I'm safe, and if it's cool I'm going wash my (peach emoji).

Big Sis: Bitch (Middle finger emoji)

Throwing my phone on the bed I stripped out of my clothes then walked to the bathroom to prepare for my shower. As the steam took over the bathroom, I quickly unbraided my hair and stepped into the hot water. As I shampooed my hair with the Kukui oil shampoo, my thoughts were invaded by those shockingly blue eyes. I had been successfully avoiding Sage for months, but today his aggression did something to me. That nigga literally had me dripping! And baaaaby the rumors about white boys having small dicks, was a blatant lie. Sage was packing like a bitch going to spring break. Grabbing my Bath and Body Works Tahiti Island Dream body wash, I lathered my body up but couldn't shake thoughts of Sage's hand exploring my body. Touching myself just wouldn't do tonight. After rinsing my hair and body off, I found myself sitting on my bed wrapped in a bath towel and scrolling through my contacts. Shockingly, none of my jump-offs would do either.

"Where is it? Where is it?" I asked aloud looking under the bed for the scrap of paper I had.

Running down the stairs I found the paper sitting on top of the counter and ran back upstairs. In a pair of PINK tights, a sports bra, a PINK jacket and a pair of UGGS I was out the door. Laughing at my "I'm going get some dick" attire, I punched the address in my GPS and was on my way to Sage's house. It ran across my mind that he may have company, but still I continued on the fifteen-minute drive to him. Pulling up, I let out a sign of relief when I noticed all the lights were off and only his flashy ass car was here.

"Ok Mizanii, no strings attached. Absolutely no strings attached. Get your nut and get out," I spoke aloud to myself as I walked up to the front door.

I looked around and noticed he had the only house on the street. Ringing the doorbell, I waited a few moments then started back to my car. I knew he had a few houses so maybe this wasn't where he slept tonight. Just as I made it to my car, I heard the sound of the door opening.

"Bring your ass in here; I knew you would show up sooner or later," he said from behind me. Spinning around my eyes damn near popped out of my head when I realized he was butt ass naked. I'm talking not even a pair of boxers. My eyes roamed his body until they landed on the midget leg he called a dick. I dropped my keys in shock, I mean I know I held it earlier but damn it was so pretty. I heard him chuckle then in just a pair of Nike slides this nigga came outside, grabbed my keys, locked my doors then carried me inside of his house.

"Sage, I—" I tried to explain why I popped up at his house unannounced but he quickly killed that noise.

"You came to fuck. Shit, I'm with it," he said, carrying me up the stairs. The way he was holding me had his dick rubbing against my pussy with every step he took and it was taking everything in me not to fuck him on this staircase. I couldn't stop myself from laughing when we got to his room. His ass had a seventy-two-inch flat screen with porn on, it was frozen so I assumed he paused it.

"What's funny? I was about to get me but since you're here you can get me instead," he said, laying me on the bed and pulling my UGGZ off. At this point, his dick was standing at attention and I swear I wanted to wrap my lips around it in the worse way. It wasn't all pink like I expected. In fact, it was tanned in comparison to the rest of his body and that had me a little confused. Before I could think about the reason why, he had removed my panties and shorts in one fluid motion. I slipped my jacket off as he freed my breast from the sports bra. Standing in between my legs he hungrily attacked them both. There was no way I could focus on what he was doing up here when his dick was sliding in and out of the folds of my pussy. He never let it slip all the way in, just casually rubbed it along my slit. Abandoning my breast, he trailed kissed up my chest until his lips found mine. I wanted him to kiss me like he did earlier. I need him to kiss me that way. I had never felt so wanted like I did when he spread my lips and caressed my tongue with his.

"Mhhmmmm," I moaned against his lips as his dick sunk further into my folds. The sounds my pussy was making made me even wetter and aided in him sliding in as he assaulted my mouth. "Noooo!" I cried out when he stepped back and started tracing kisses from my stomach down to my thighs. The kisses were soft, sensual, completely unexpected from him. Making his way in between my thighs, he started this pattern of kissing my inner thighs then sucking the same area, no doubt leaving his mark. Just when I thought I couldn't take it anymore, he allowed his tongue to graze my pussy in the most intimate of ways. The graze was so soft if I didn't see him doing it I may have missed it. That only caused my pussy to anticipate him more.

"Damn ma, you smell so fucking good," he moaned damn near sticking his nose in my pussy and sniffing. "And you are so fucking wet," he said as he dove head first into my dripping pussy. The sensitivity went out the window and was replaced with the aggression that I had been anticipating. My legs began shaking as he alternated between licking my pussy and sucking on my clit. It didn't take long before my eyes crossed and he was slurping up my juices. For the first time in forever, I was satisfied with the head. Before I could catch my breath, I felt his dick invading my insides. Sage took his time with my body, slowly entering me as his hand rested underneath me gently touching my back. Once inside he stopped for a second so that I could get used to his size. I had never had someone be so gentle yet aggressive, as if I might break if he stroked too deep or hard. After a few seconds, he fucked me nice and slow. Like he was learning my body and studying my curves. I was never the type to make love but I wanted this. I needed this. The feeling of his monster deep inside of me and his balls softly tapping my ass caused me to squirt all over his dick and lower stomach. What took me by surprise was the tear that escaped my eye.

"Don't tell me you getting soft on me. I thought I would hit you with the Lifetime dick you were so worried about, but let's go BET now." He laughed, flipping me over. Before I could form words, he was entering me from the back. Grabbing my waist, he started hitting me with long strokes that had me clenching my stomach muscles. There was no way in hell I should be feeling him here. Trying to catch some form of break, I threw my right arm behind me to slow his attempt at punishing my pussy. This was a big mistake. He quickly grabbed that arm then the other and held them behind me. Using my arms, he pulled my body back to match him thrust for thrust.

"Ohhhhhhh SAGGGGE! FUCKKK MEEEE!" I yelled out as he worked my pussy. I felt my pussy juices leaking down my thigh and that only added to my excitement. Throwing it back on him it was his turn to try to control the situation as he dropped my arms and grabbed my waist.

WHAP!

The slap to my ass caused a pleasurable sting as I found myself once again nutting. I felt Sage push down on my back causing me to arch even further as his dick slid deeper.

"OOOHH SHIT! OOOOOHHHH SHIT! Sage hold on!" I begged as he fucked me while I was still shaking from the orgasm. I felt his strokes slow down a little and the throbbing of his dick let me know he would be nutting right behind me. Looking over my shoulder I watched as his face got stuck in what I thought was the sexiest face ever. Moments later, I felt him filling up the condom as he collapsed on my back with his dick still inside of me. After catching our breaths everything in me said get up and go home, but instead I rolled over and dozed off.

Chapter 13:

Dynastii

I ignored the ringing of my phone once again as I tried to complete this online test. I was finally back in school after Tec made it perfectly clear that I wouldn't be involved in street shit. At first, I was completely against the idea but he has been holding up his end of the bargain. He had been combing the streets to find out who would want to touch my baby. In the short amount of time that Amir and I have been dating, I've found in him what I didn't even know I was missing in Prez. He was supportive of the fact that I didn't want the street life, hell he didn't want the street life and he was really the 'president to the streets'. This shit wasn't just some name given to him, he lived that life and earned the name. He was so understanding, there were many nights when I would wake up crying because Malakhi came to me in a dream. Instead of getting aggravated he would hold me, rock me, or just whatever I needed. One time he actually came with me to the graveyard at three in the morning when I couldn't sleep. He was everything I didn't know I needed.

Answering the last question with five minutes to spare I felt confident in my work. Amir had made me flash cards a few nights ago and we went over them daily so the test wasn't as challenging as I thought it would be. Jumping up I decided to get a start on dinner before Amir showed up acting like he was starving. Just as I made it to the kitchen, my phone started ringing again. Spinning around I snatched it and answered before the caller disconnected.

"Hello?"

"Yes, is this, Dynastii?" asked a soft voice.

"Yeah this is she. Who is this?" I asked, stuffing the phone between my ear and my shoulder blade.

"You don't know me but we should talk, soon."

"About what exactly?" I questioned.

"I have some information you may want on President and Ashanti. But only if the price is right," she said with no shame in her game. I immediately started laughing.

"Honey, I can assure you the price is most definitely not right. In fact, its flat out wrong. You can't tell me anything about those two that I one, don't already know or two, don't care to know," I said literally unbothered.

"You sure about that?" she asked and I didn't care for the tone of her voice.

"Positive. I didn't catch your name, what did you say it was?" I asked.

"I didn't throw it. You have a lovely evening, Dynastii. Oh, and I'm sorry about what happened to Malakhi," she said.

"Wait, how do you know my son's name? What do you know about him?" I screamed but it was too late. She had already hung up the phone. I tried to dial her back but the call was restricted. "Fuck, Fuck, Fuck!" I screamed throwing my phone across the room just as Amir and Sage walked in.

"Baby, what's wrong?" Amir rushed to my side as Sage cocked his gun. Not wanting to be weak in front of Sage I ran up the stairs and to the bedroom where I knew Amir would follow. We had this rule, while in the comforts of our room we were able to relax. We were able just to be ourselves with no judgement. I fell to my knees with tears pouring from my face as he rushed into the room. Lifting me from the floor, he pulled me into his arms.

"Shhh, shhh. Tell me what's going on. Why are you crying?" he asked, running his fingers through my hair.

"Someone called my phone and said she had information I would want to know. I told her I didn't but before she hung up she mentioned my son. What if I fucked it up and she had the answers that I needed?" I cried.

"Dynastii, look at me, I need you to stop letting this consume your life, ma. I know you want justice for lil' man, shit I want justice for lil' man too, but you can't let that eat you alive. That blocked call I can get that traced, ma that ain't shit but what I can't do is let you drive yourself crazy over this. We going get some answers and sooner rather than later." He grabbed my chin and made me look him in the eyes. "You trust me? And don't just say yes, think about it. Do you trust me?" he asked.

"With my life," I answered without hesitation. "I don't need time to think about that because I've been thinking about that very thing for months. I knew I trusted you when you told me enroll into school and get out the streets because you had it covered. Nothing Prez said could make me wait on him to handle shit. I knew I trusted you a long time ago," I confessed.

"Speaking of Prez, I have something to tell you. It may hurt you and I apologize in advance for having to be the one to bring this to you." The way his voice lowered let me know what he wanted to say. I saw the pain in his eyes. I knew the digging through Prez's business would uncover the secrets he and Ashanti thought they buried.

"What's that?" I asked.

"Remember I thought Ashanti's baby was mine? Well I found out who the father is—" he said before I cut him off.

"Yeah, It's Prez," I said, wiping the stray tear that fell. "I found out when she arrived at visitation the same time I was there. That's where I was coming from the day I met you here. As a matter of fact, the caller initially said she had info on those two."

"I'm going find out who that was, don't trip. How was your test, I know you aced that bitch!" he said with excitement in his voice. It never failed, he always got so excited when we discussed anything to do with my future. I don't know if what I felt for him was love just yet, but I was deeply infatuated with him.

"You know I did, so I'll be expecting my gift." I laughed, shaking my Pandora bracelet in his face. Every time I aced a test, Amir would give me another piece of jewelry.

"You know I got you. But check this out, I need you to get dressed real quick. We have to make a run," he said with a huge smile on his face.

"Ok, where are we going?" I asked, walking to the closet.

"Why can't you just get dressed nosey ass girl?" he asked as he walked to the bathroom and turned on the shower.

"Well I need to know if I need to casually kill them or leave bloody footsteps once I leave the murder scene." I laughed.

"What the hell are you talking about, son?" he asked as I continued to laugh at my own joke.

"Do I need to dress up or nah?" I asked in English.

"Go hop in the shower and let me pick out your clothes," he suggested. Shrugging my shoulders, I did as he said. I wasn't concerned with him selecting my clothing because Amir had excellent taste in clothing.

Pressing play on the iPod deck in the bathroom, the sounds of Patti Labelle surrounded me. Amir always laughed because my taste in music was all over. I went from Future to Monica to Webbie and back to Anita if I felt like it. Stripping from Amir's boxers and muscle shirt I stepped into the free-falling shower and let the hot water cascade down my frame. It had been a while since I washed my hair so I decided to get that out the way as I sang along with Patti.

"I must have rehearsed my lines, a thousand times,

Until I had them memorized..."

"Ahh!" I screamed before I realized the arms that wrapped around my waist were Amir's.

"Don't stop, sing to my while I wash your hair ma." He said squeezing shampoo in his hand as I tilted my head back so he could work his magic. This was nothing new, in fact, I looked forward to the times when he would pamper me; which were often. Now I swear to you I couldn't sing to save anyone's life but Amir always listened like I was Beyoncé.

After washing my hair, Amir grabbed my loofah and slowly cleaned my body from head to toe. He had showered before he left an hour ago so I knew this was all to cater to me. Amir truly represented everything that was good in a man. I know there was no such thing as perfect, but he ran a damn close race. After Amir dried me off, I walked into my room and smiled at the clothing he chose. On the bed was a crème colored long sleeve tee that left my back completely exposed, a pair of distressed Fashion Nova skinny jeans and sitting on the floor next to the bed were a pair of metallic gold Giuseppe Zanotti Cruel Summer Sandals. After wearing a pair for dinner, his ass went get me every color because they were so fly, in his words.

Walking to my vanity I lightly beat my face, then secured my tresses with a French braid that swept the top of my ass. I slipped on my clothes and then threw on the jewelry he left on the bed.

"DAMN!" He said walking out of the closed matching my fly in a crème colored V-neck t-shirt that faded to black, some light wash True Religion jeans and a pair of black and gold Balenciaga high tops. He was shining with his gold Cuban link chain and matching bracelet. I already knew the look that graced my face when he started shaking his head.

"Nope! We goin' handle that later, yo ass goin' have us late, ma." I laughed, grabbing my Birkin bag and followed him out the door. Walking outside I started cheesing as I looked at the stretch Hummer that was going to take us to our destination.

"Where are we going, Amir?" I asked again. "And where did Sage go?" I just remembered he had walked in with Amir.

"Mind your business, Dynastii," he said, holding a chocolate covered strawberry to my lips as we cruised the city in the limo. Taking a bite, I couldn't help but to smile that this man was all mine. Holding a champagne flute to my lips, I downed the best tasting champagne I had ever tasted then asked for more. We made small talk for a while before I dozed off. School had been kicking my ass. The flashing of lights woke me up. Opening my eyes, I was surrounding by my family posing for pictures around me.

"Oh shit, she's up," Sage said, saving his camera.

"I'm going fuck your white ass up, Sage," I said, wiping the sides of my mouth.

"Oh, I already caught the money shot with the drool, ma. You gotta pay my white ass to get rid of it," he said, causing me to laugh before I full got a look around.

"Are we on a damn plane?" I asked panicking. I watched too much *Final Destination* and I wasn't beat for this shit. "Oh, hell naw!" I said as everyone laughed. Suddenly I felt a squeeze on my hand and looked to my left where Amir was smiling.

"I got you ma, calm down. Nothing is going happen to your scary ass. I'll fuck the pilot up if he makes us wreck and mess up your face and shit," he said, causing me to laugh. Leave it to Amir's ass."

"Where are we going, Amir" I asked.

"You'll see in a minute, we should be landing soon." He smirked.

"How long have we been on this plane?" I questioned.

"Like five hours." Now I was puzzled, I know I was sleepy but a five-hour nap was overkill.

"And I slept that long?" I wondered aloud.

"With a lil' help." Before I could ask Amir's ass if he drugged me the pilot came on over the intercom.

"Ladies and Gentlemen I first want to say happy early birthday to Ms. Dynastii. I hope you enjoy Vegas, look out your window and thanks for flying Air Amir." He said as I looked out the window then froze.

"You have your own plane?" I asked as he nodded. All I could do was laugh. Here it was I thought my boyfriend was modest but this nigga owned his own plane. After an easy landing, we grabbed our luggage then took a limo to The MGM Grand, where we would be staying. This hotel was amazing but I had no time to look at that, I was already ready to hit the malls.

Chapter 14:

The turn up for Dynastii's birthday was real! Amir spared no expenses to make sure she enjoyed herself. It was day six of our seven- night stay and we were currently turning up at Rehab's pool party.

"You just going sit here and not got that sexy body wet?" Sage asked, walking over to me. I had to lick my lips as the water dropped down his abs. Sage ass knew he was the shit.

"I stay wet Sage; you should know that from experience." I laughed once I noticed his dick started bricking up. Since I showed up at his house, I had been avoiding having sex with him, that shit was addictive. I found myself wondering what he was up to, what was he doing, and who was he doing it with way too often.

"Yeah I'm trying to backstroke back in that thang, but you playing," he said, stepping in my personal space and wrapping his arm around my waist.

"I don't know why y'all two play these games with each other. Just make that shit official," Dynastii said, walking up with two drinks in her hand. You could tell she was having the time of her life; her smile was contagious.

"Girl, Sage doesn't know what to do with a woman like me. He wouldn't know how to handle all of this on a daily basis." I passed my hand down my curves that were on full display in the one-piece thong bathing suit. I had attempted to cover up with a sarong but lost it when I noticed that over 80% of the women were wearing the same damn thing.

"Yeah, alright keep telling yourself that like I didn't already show and prove," Sage replied, walking back to where Amir was bobbing his head to the live concert.

"Z, what's so bad with giving him a chance? You know that man loves your ass." Dynastii asked, looking at me over her shades.

"That's the fucking problem, I think I fell for him too. You know I don't do relationships, Dynastii. I don't know the first thing about being exclusively with someone. And his ass made it perfectly clear that he wasn't being my jump off. You know while y'all were playing sports in school I was playing niggas," I honestly answered.

"You know what you're right. If Sage is anything like Amir, he goin' kill your ass for playing him." She laughed. "You know we leave tomorrow, what y'all wanna do for our last night here?" she asked.

"Shit, we did damn near everything there was to do out here. Anyway, Tec told us don't make plans with you. He wants you to himself tonight. We actually have a spa trip with the girls in about an hour and a half," I said, winking at her. Tec had an amazing night planned for them and I was so excited my sister got to experience love like this.

"Oh really?" she asked with excitement dancing in her eyes. "Oh well we need to go, let me get my man cause he ain't staying with all these naked women," she said, walking away. I watched as she tapped Tec and whispered in his ear. My face frowned up when Tec shook up with Sage and they walked towards us with Serenity and Amor following. "Let's go," Dynastii said once they were back in front of me.

"Umm, why is Sage still over there?" I asked as a female walked up and engaged in conversation with him.

"He said he was going chill for a lil' longer," Tec answered. Downing the rest of my drink I stood to my feet.

"No he ain't. We came together so he leaving with us," I said, making my way over to where he was talking to the female near the pool. I listened as the chick asked why he blocked her number and that she needed to talk to him.

"Zeke the freak it is time to go," I cut in. The whole situation reminded me of *Think Like a Man 2*, when Zeke ran into a woman he fucked with a while back. Like we we're way in Vegas, why are your thotties here too?" Hearing my voice, he turned to me and his face immediately broke out in a grin.

"I knew your sister wasn't the only territorial one. You ain't want my fine ass out here alone, huh?" he asked before turning to the female. "Cheyenne, be safe out here shorty. I'm going dip with wifey," he said before following me away. I caught the look she sent my way and ignored her ass.

WHAP

"What the fuck, Sage!" I said, hitting him for slapping my ass.

"Nobody told you to have my shit on display, ma. Here!" he said handing me the sarong to cover up with. I tied it around my waist then picked up his shirt.

"Here you go too then." I said as he threw the V-Neck on over his swim trunks. We met up with the crew and the men and women went their separate ways.

***

"My damn key card isn't working," I complained to the front desk. After all the pampering that we had just received, I was ready to lay down but I couldn't.

"Let me see your card please," the attendant asked extending her hand towards me. After a few brushes of her keyboard, she issued me a different card with a smile.

"Your room was upgraded to one of our best suites. Your bags are already waiting for you up there. I wanted to question it but she just said a better suite, for free, I'm with it.

After getting lost in this huge hotel, I was finally standing outside of my room. Even the damn doorknob was fancier. Sliding my key card, the smell of lavender hit me at the door. The plush carpet was so brilliantly white I didn't hesitate to remove my shoes at the door. Walking in, I admired the sitting area and kitchen layout. I ventured in further until I laid eyes on the magnificent room. This was something I could surely get used to. Walking over to the bed I grabbed the letter that I thought came from the hotel and couldn't help but smile.

Mizanii,

Look, don't start yo shit nah. I want to pamper you even better than they did at the expensive ass spa, and that shit was expensive. I think you owe me some more ass after all the charges I saw appear. Anyway, go ahead and get in the bathtub. I ran your water and I have some wine and shit in there for you. Mizanii, I ain't playing with yo ass, I don't want no lip.

Enjoy,

Sage.

The smile I had refused to leave my face. I stripped out of my maxi dress and panties then walked into the spacious bathroom. The more I walked around this mini apartment, the more I wanted to extend this trip. Next to the tub was a plush pink robe with a note that said, *Wear me after you wash your ass.* Something was really wrong with that child. I couldn't help but to laugh as I sunk into the warm bath water. The bubble bath smelled amazing and I must have dozed off. Because when I woke up Lavender wasn't the only thing I was smelling. I quickly bathe myself, dried off and slipped on the robe. Stepping into the room, that smile made another appearance.

"Took you long enough, I almost ate your food," Sage said, standing near the table in the kitchen with a suit jacket over a muscle shirt and boxers.

"Sage, what are you wearing?" I laughed.

"Shit this is my formal wear. Come sit down so I can feed you," he said, extending his hand out. Grabbing his hand, I sat in the chair he pulled out for me.

"Where is your plate?" I asked, noticing only one plate.

"This is all about you, ma," he said before he proceeded to feed me the lobster, shrimp, potatoes and asparagus. The meal was amazing and if I were alone I would have wanted a second serving. "If you're still hungry later I'll warm you some then," he said reading my mind and helping me up. We walked to the room and I watched as he stripped butt ass naked then untied my robe.

"You're not getting any ass, Sage." I laughed only half serious.

"I'm not on that, at least not at the moment." He smirked. "We're going in the hot tub," he said, opening the door to the balcony. The view was amazing, we could see everything but no one could see us. I stepped in as he stepped away and returned with a bottle of Henny and two glasses. Sage knew I wasn't the wine and champagne type and I appreciated that.

"This is nice and unexpected, Sage," I said, accepting my glass as he stepped in with that monster swinging.

"I could treat you like this all the time if your ass would give me a chance," he said, throwing back his shot. Following his lead, I threw mine back and poured us another.

"A chance at what, being my man? Loving me?" I paused as he nodded his head up and down. "That's cute and all but I ain't cut out to be in a relationship. I'm like Tiara Thomas on that Wale track. I can't promise that I'll be good to you. Why can't we just continue fucking and going about our business?" I asked, taking another shot.

"You may want to slow down on those shots. You know your ass is a lightweight. Anyway, I feel like I'm the perfect person to show you how to commit. Don't think on that too much tonight, though," he said as I stared into his blue eyes.

"Why did your parents name you, Sage?" I asked the question I've wanted to know for a while before taking another shot.

"Because of my eye color," he answered.

"But Sage is green and your eyes are blue," I informed him, looking confused.

"My mama was a crackhead, I know you going mind your business. If she thought, they were green then them bitches green," he said as we both fell out laughing. "Aye, let's play truth or dare. If you don't follow through on your dares you have to take two shots," He suggested. Never one to back down from a challenge I agreed, which was a big mistake.

Chapter 15:

Sage

"What's good y'all?" I asked, dabbing Tec and pulling Serenity, Amore and Dynastii in for a hug.

"Shit, nigga how is it that your ass glowing. I thought that was the woman's role in a fresh marriage?" Tec said, laughing.

"Yeah, marriage looks good on you. Speaking of which, where is your wife anyway?" Dynastii asked.

"Mizanii will be here in a few with her mad ass. She may as well get used to it cause ain't no divorce, bih," I said dead ass serious.

"But y'all did get married during a drunken night in Vegas, son." Tec said, causing me to look at him.

"Nigga, I was tipsy so I knew what I was doing. Her ass was drunk but that ain't stop her from walking out that chapel screaming "I's married nah," I said, mocking my wife's drunk voice. It had been two days since we came back Vegas, two days since Mizanii woke up sober and as my wife. After a bottle of Hennessey and a game of truth or dare, we went to a chapel and tied the knot. That shit wasn't even on me either, her drunk ass dared me to marry her. I've been saying since the jump that she was my wife so I did that shit. I ran out and brought her a fat ass rock, and helped her get into a simple white dress. In basketball shorts, a muscle shirt, a blazer and Gucci slides, a nigga said I do. We got married by Michael Jackson and Whitney Houston, looking back on everything, that shit was hella funny.

"So, what are y'all going do about y'all living arrangements?" Tec asked.

"I took care of them."

"How?" He questioned.

"You'll see shortly," I assured him as I walked to the kitchen. "What you cooking in here Dynastii? The shit smells good," I complimented.

"Nothing impressive. Lasagna and garlic knots, oh and a side salad," she answered.

"Oh, Tec got your ass hooking up his favorite shit, huh. I asked your sister to hook up my favorite food and her mean ass told me she 'd season it with rat poison. She didn't laugh or anything, her ass is evil," I said.

"Yeah and I don't think you should take that lightly. Her ass was serious and she's a lil' bit crazy. I really think you're good for her though. I mean let's be honest this marriage thing came left field and is really unconventional; but I still see this being a good thing for you both."

"Make sure you tell her that when she comes in here ready to kill me, ok. She had some appointment today for some shit called Goddess Locks, so no telling how long she'll be," I said.

"What the hell did you do now?"

"I moved some things around, you know she trips for anything though." I smiled as I walked back outside near the pool where everyone else was. After about thirty minutes, we were all on the outside patio eating and talking when Mizanii made her appearance.

"Sage, I'm going fuck you up. Where is all my shit!" she screamed, walking to the backyard.

"Hello to you too wifey, I love your hair," I said, stuffing my mouth.

"Sage, watch I shoot your ass right in those fake ass green eyes. Where is my shit man?" she asked again.

"What's going on, Mizanii?" Dynastii asked her.

"So, I go to my house before I got my hair done right, nothing is wrong. Everything is perfectly in place. I leave my fully furnished home for a few hours to get my hair done and when I get back there is nothing in my house. NOTHING! Even the damn blinds are gone," she said before pointing in my face. "And I know it's his ass because he's been saying his wife would live under the same roof as him. This is his way of getting me to leave my house," she said, causing me to laugh.

"You know how sexy you are when you're mad? I told you I hate being alone, asked Tec. I've been that way, now I don't have to be. I have a wife." I winked and walked in the house to save my plate.

"Sage, we talked about this. The wedding wasn't even real; we have to date before we're married," she said, following me in the house.

"Who said that, Mizanii? I feel like it was real, I have the pictures to prove it," I said, pulling out my wallet that housed a picture of she and I along with Michael and Whitney.

"If you show me that picture again I swear I will fuck you up. Where is all of my things?"

"I saved them in a storage. If you can give us an honest chance and it doesn't work, then I'll give it back. Other than that, I'll see you at home, wifey," I said, kissing her on the cheek. "Your handprint is programmed in the system; I'll be home before seven." Mizanii can play all she wants too but she married to my fine ass and I don't believe in divorce.

Chapter 16:

Chloe

I know I was worth more than just a mention, right? Yeah, I know I was introduced as Ashanti's best friend but that couldn't be further from the truth. At one point, I did consider her my best friend, I loved Ashanti like a sister but have you ever tried to hug a poisonous snake? The bitch bites you, hard.

My mother was this weak-minded white woman before she drunk herself into her early grave. At a young age, she fell in love with and married my father, the illegitimate son to a street king. Because he was his father's best kept secret he was very well off. Adding to that, he began practicing law and had crooked judges, lawyers and politicians all in his pockets. Our money was longer than a Brazilian bitch's hair. My mother however, wasn't there for the money. She loved my father through the abuse, the recreational drugs he used, and the late nights when the sun would beat him home. We both did, my father was a king in my eyes, and he treated me like I was his princess. There was never a time that I could remember him coming in the house empty handed. I could always count on a surprise gift from him. The love he showed me made everyone jealous, sometimes even my mother. So, imagine my surprise when he decided he wanted to leave my mother while I was in my junior year of high school.

My teenage heart was shattered when my mother packed up and we left in the middle of the night. When we first moved, I begged and I begged for an explanation but never received one. Because the phones were in my mom's name and she disconnected my father's number, I couldn't reach out to him. My mother's number never changed though and according to her, he never reached out to me. She had moved me clear across the country and that had damn near eaten away at her savings. Therefore, the poor little mixed girl was thrown into an urban high school where all friendships and bonds had been made. I hated my situation, my mother, and my father. Through it all, I stayed in touch with my then best friend, Ashanti. I wound up dropping out of school and got a job to pay the bills, since my mother decided that being a full-time drunk would be her new occupation. One night while working my neighbor called me to tell me I needed to come get my mother from her apartment. She had gotten so drunk she wandered in the wrong apartment and was asleep in their bed. You know they say a drunken tongue speaks the truth. I'll never forget when I found out Ashanti was the reason my life had drastically changed.

"I'm so sorry about this Ms. Robertson. Thanks for calling me." I said as soon as my neighbor opened her door.

"Uh huh, whenever she sobers up please let her know this can't happen again. I had company tonight," she said, tightening her silk robe, I noticed she was naked underneath. If I weren't so pissed that I had to leave my job at Subway, I would have laughed. Ms. Robertson was getting her freak on.

"Yes ma'am. Again, I apologize, where is she?" I asked, following her to the master bedroom where I could smell the liquor permeating from my mother's body from the door. Embarrassingly, I woke her up and got her next door to our apartment. Before I left for work this morning I made sure the apartment was spotless. Looking around I could tell some of her friends came over because there was a stench in the air and liquor bottles of all sort thrown around. After getting her in the bed and showering, I went clean the living room until my phone started ringing.

"Hello." I answered on the first ring.

"What's wrong now?" Ashanti asked sensing my frustration. As soon as she asked that one question the flood gates opened.

"Ashanti, I can't do this anymore. I'm working twenty-four fucking seven and still go without eating on some days because of these bills. My mama is getting worst, and this apartment is bullshit. I need a change, man," I said, crying.

"Chloe, I live alone now, just come here."

"Wait are you serious, you aren't even eighteen yet." I gasped.

"It's not in my name. My man got it for me," she replied.

"Really, you're seeing someone new? Who is he?" I asked.

"Actually, I would rather not answer that just yet. I don't want to jinx a fresh relationship. But like I was saying you have somewhere else to go, you know my house is always open. And you don't have to pay anything, my man covers it." She laughed.

"Ashanti, are you sure?" I asked with excitement filling my voice. "It would only be for a little while, just until I can get on my feet." I assured her.

"Yeah girl that's fine, just let me know when you decide to come."

"I don't know what to say to my mama but something has to shake. I think I'll put her in rehab. Let me call you back after I talk it over with her," I said before hanging up.

"Talk what over with me?" I heard from behind me. Spinning around I saw my mother with a bottle of brown liquor to her mouth. This made my decision that much easier and I decided to use tough love on her.

"Mama I'm going back home, you can either stay here and drink your life away or let me get you into rehab. The choice is yours, either way I'm leaving. I don't know what happened to you. You let a man break you and leave you out here drunk, pathetic, and hopeless," I said with all the strength I could muster. "Ashanti told me I can move in with her, so that's what I'm going to do." I didn't expect the laughter to follow.

"Oh, you moving with Ashanti, huh? And will her and your

father scoot over so you can slide in the bed with them?" she asked in a drunken slur, causing me to frown in confusion.

"What the hell are you talking about?" I asked, refusing to believe what my brain was trying to tell me.

"Your father leaving didn't break me. It's the fact that your fucking father became a pedophile. I didn't leave him! He left us for that seventeen-year-old tramp bitch!" she spat, causing tears to fall from my eyes. My best friend knew how much my father meant to me and this is how she repays me? She broke up my fucking family. "So run to them, maybe your father loves you enough to leave her cause he damn sure didn't love me enough. You can go, I'm used to people leaving, I'll sign whatever papers I need to," she said, breaking the bottle as she threw it to the floor and walked back to her room.

It was at that moment that I began operation ruin Ashanti. She had to pay for all she did to me. It kills me that when I moved in with her my father would sneak in and out her room when he thought I was asleep. He never cared to stop in and see me and he knew I was living there. They both had to pay. I got him already, but Ashanti I played with for years. I slept with each and everyone her boyfriends, except Prez and Amir. She never understood why they didn't stick around but it was because of me. I made them fall for me and they became my sponsors. I was working on permanently ending her and Prez though. I wanted him for myself. I was done playing games with Ashanti, I wanted her dead. I tried to call Dynastii and make her do my dirty work but the shit flopped, that bitch truly didn't care. Oh well, plan B in full effect and I ain't talking contraceptives.

Chapter 17:

Ashanti

Tapping away on the screen of my iPhone 7, I sent Amir yet another message. I hated being ignored, especially by him. For years, I had him wrapped around my finger and all it took was for one bitch to come fuck this up for me. I looked up just in time to see Chloe's Range Rover pulling up in front of the valet.

"It's about time you showed up; I've been here for thirty minutes," I told Chloe while rolling my eyes as she walked up.

"Well, all of this beauty takes time," she said, causing me to stare at her in envy. Her small frame looked amazing in the flowy jumpsuit she was rocking. It hugged her curves just right, and gave her a sophisticated look. Her makeup was impeccably applied and the top knot she wore her hair in let her beautiful features shine through. I didn't say anything as she removed her shades and took a seat. "You okay, you looking like you have a problem?" she asked with a smile on her face.

"I'm good just stressing over my men problems." I replied.

"Oh, that's why you look so bad off. You shouldn't stress it's not good for your skin," she said as she threw mad shade.

To say I helped her ass out of a tough spot, she had surely changed once she moved back with me. I used to feel guilty for the secret I kept from her. That was my main reason for allowing her to move with me. Shit, she was damn near paying for my house, it was rightfully hers but she'd never know. I didn't mean to fall in love with Hilton. Her father and I fucking around was supposed to be a one-time thing but the money was good and the dick was even better. Did I feel bad for being the cause of her parents being divorced, no. I didn't tell her dad to leave or her mom to be so damn weak. Everything that happened was completely their fault.

"Chloe, I'm being serious," I said, rolling my eyes. "I don't know what to do; my life is literally falling apart."

"What's the problem now, you appear to be perfectly fine to be honest."

"That bitch Dynastii really has gotten in Amir's ear. He told me he would stop by my house to drop off an application to his furniture shop. He actually wants me to work for my money. And he knew my bills were due and refused to pay them. He won't even take my calls, in fact when I last called he made Dynastii tell me to stop calling his phone. What does she have over me?" I cried.

"I don't know why you're so mad, you took her man and she took yours."

"Speaking of which, Prez is working on my nerves too," I confessed.

"What is he doing?" she asked before we paused to place our drink orders.

"I love Prez, or so I thought. But as more and more time goes by I feel like this ain't what I need. There is no telling how long he will be locked up. The money I was holding for him is running low."

"Wait, so you have money for Prez, a nigga that's seeing football numbers. You mean to tell me you're suffering and talking about finding a job and you have his funds in your possession. Bitch, if you don't live off of that, I know it's enough money until you find a come up," she said, causing me to immediately shake my head no.

"I can't touch that money, Prez will kill me. He needs that for when he touches down." I stopped explaining when I saw the way she was looking at me.

"Prez has you in a fucked-up ass position first of all. He owes you! Stop accepting those damn calls. He is playing you! I didn't want to hurt your feelings but when I went visit my friend in jail Dynastii and him looked real friendly. I'm actually glad you've already started missing visitations," She said as our mimosas were placed in front of us. I felt my heart shattering.

"What does this bitch have over me?" I loudly repeated again, scaring the waitress.

"Are y'all ready to order?" she asked.

"No just keep my mimosas coming, I think I just lost my appetite." I sat in my thoughts as Chloe placed her order. Maybe she had a point. I was sitting on enough of Prez's money to live the life I was used to for a while. I needed to get Dynastii away from my ATM though. Then it hit me.

"Umm Chloe, I need your help," I said.

"With what, you know I don't lend out money," she said, causing me to kiss my teeth.

"I need to get Dynastii away from Amir. What can I do?" I asked.

"Oh, that's simple. A chick like that won't tolerate cheating. When he drops the application off, fuck him. Then take a picture or video and make sure she sees it," she said while looking at her phone.

"That's it?" I ask not really convinced.

"Baby when a bitch doesn't need a man, she won't accept any of his bullshit, that I can guarantee you. She can bounce on his ass and I promise you her life will move on the same way. As for Prez, stop answering those calls and take care of my godchild," she said, making complete sense. Now the problem was getting Amir in my bed. Amir was not the cheating type so it would take some extreme scheming to get him to even take a whiff of the pussy. After a few drinks, I was on the way home to get my son. Just as I pulled in the yard, Prez called.

"How can I help you today, Prez?" I asked with attitude evident in my voice.

"Why the fuck did you miss visitation today?" he asked, no hey, hello or how are you. Instead of telling the truth, I decided to test him.

"Your child was sick so I've been busy with him," I said.

"Well couldn't you have taken him to the hospital after you came see me? You've missed quite a few visits now. I have needs!" he roared damn near pissing me off. He knew I would do anything for my son. After past experiences a simple cough from my son scared me, he knew this. He of all people should have respected that. I knew then Chloe was on the right track.

"You wanted me to put our son to the side so that you could get some pussy?" I asked to confirm.

"When you say it that way it seems fucked up." He said like the shit wasn't fucked up in every motherfucking language.

"So what way do you want me to say it so it sounds better, huh? Cause it seemed real fucking fucked up when you let those words come from your mouth. You didn't get enough of Dynastii when she was there?" I asked, feeling myself getting jealous.

"What the fuck are you talking about?" he asked, pissing me off.

"You can play stupid if you want to but whatever. You do what you want to do and I'll do what I have to do," I said, hanging up on him.

Walking in the house, I paid the sitter then went sit with my son. I watched as he napped and a smile crossed my face. He was growing so much and all I wanted was for his father to love him. I didn't understand why that was too much to ask for. Sitting there listening to his snores I came up with a plan to get Amir back. If he couldn't have his father's love, he'll have to settle for Amir's.

Chapter 18:

Tec

"No wonder I was so damn warm." I laughed as I woke up to Dynastii's naked body wrapped around me.

Last night she made the decision to sleep at her home but obviously, that didn't go as planned. I don't know why she let the words, sleeping apart, run through her mind. She enjoyed sleeping with me as much as I enjoyed sleeping with her. Slipping out of bed, I looked back and notice she didn't stir at the sudden movement. After taking care of my hygiene, I slipped in my closet and searched for my clothing for the day. I decided on a plain black polo V-neck, a pair of white True Religion jeans and a pair of black Balenciaga high top sneakers, then was out the door.

After checking on money and a quick stop, I arrived at the graveyard. I grabbed the bag and stopped at the first grave, Malakhi's. I had never gotten a chance to meet him but anytime I came run it with my brother, I stopped and talked to lil' man. I was in love with his mama, so how could I ignore him. I pulled out the NASCAR collector's cars I had for him and lined them along his headstone.

"What's up lil' man? I see your mama recently came, she still spoiling you with toys and what not." I looked around at all the toys he had and smiled. "You have a special woman as a mama. I'm going find out who placed you here so you can really rest in peace. Keep looking over your mama for me," I said before walking over to where my brother rested. I smiled at the fresh arrangement of flowers. I knew what Amor and Aunt B had dropped off but smiled harder when I noticed the same arrangement that was on Malakhi's grave. I never had to ask Dynastii, baby handled shit off the muscle. Anytime she dropped lil' man something and cleaned his grave, she did the same for Ahmad.

"Say nigga, I see my woman came through, dropped some flowers, and cleaned your spot. Don't be looking at her ass neither nigga. Check it; I came bring you your birthday gifts. If you were here we would pour up..." I paused and poured the entire bottle of D'usse around his grave. "Nigga we would roll up..." I paused again and sprinkled some loud too. "And you know your ass would want all the bitches." I laughed as I threw a pic of his favorite stripper, Cheeks, on his grave. "I love you boy. We may not have seen eye to eye all the time but you knew I was head-first behind you," I finished before kissing his headstone and bouncing. Looking at my phone, I know I needed to make one more stop before I made it home to my girl.

Sitting in the driveway, I face two blunts and calmed my nerves before getting down and banging on the door.

"I'm glad you decided to come," Ashanti said, answering the door in a black lace bodysuit that left nothing to the imagination.

Her ass, pussy, and titties were on display and I would be lying if a nigga said his dick didn't brick up. The thigh high boots she wore made her thick legs look as if they went on for days. She spread her legs a little so I could see that pretty pink pussy peaking from the crotchless area. I couldn't help licking my lips, its second nature to men.

"Shit, you was blowing me up so I had to see what's good. I thought there was an emergency or something," I said, pulling at my beard.

"There is an emergency, one that only you could solve. I see I have to handle a lil' emergency for you too," she said, staring at my dick that was begging to be freed. "You goin' come in or you goin' stay out there?" She asked, licking her full lips that

123

were painted red. Knowing I should have carried my ass back to the car, I followed her in. It wasn't my fault though; her ass was screaming follow me Amir, follow me. So, that's exactly what I did. My mind was on Dynastii but my dick was on something else.

"What you on right now, Ashanti?" I asked as she walked to the kitchen.

"Nothing, really. I was lounging around and you did kind of just pop in. I was trying this outfit on actually," she said, causing me to side eye her.

"Yeah, alright whatever."

"But since you're here, I did cook some lasagna and garlic bread. I know that's your favorite let me get you a plate," she said, walking to the kitchen causing that fat ass to switch behind her. My eyes followed her until I couldn't anymore. After a few moments, she came back with a healthy sized plate and a cup of Kool-Aid.

"Appreciate that, what was so important that you needed me over here?" I asked, stuffing a huge piece of lasagna in my mouth. "This shit is good. A nigga thought you forgot how to cook for a second. I remember I used to have to beg for meals." I said, downing some of the diabetic ass drink.

"We will talk after you eat." She smiled. Something told me save myself the trouble and carry my ass home to my woman.

Chapter 19:

Prez

"...97, 98, 99, 100." I counted my last few push-ups then lifted myself from the ground. Checking my surroundings, I flipped my mattress over and dug in the hole I made to house my cell phone. After powering it on, I facetimed Ashanti dumb ass.

"What can I help you with, Prez?" she answered without even looking into the camera.

"What the fuck is wrong with yo needy ass now, Ashanti?" I snapped. Lately it was always something with this bitch, she was worse than Dynastii.

"I'm watching TV and bonding with *our* son and you're bothering me." She made sure she emphasized that fucking our too. I don't know who told her or Dynastii ass that I wanted to be a father. That shit wasn't in the cards for me, fuck I didn't even have a father. As far as I was concerned when they decided to have a child, they decided to be single parents.

"Stop fucking playing with me. Why haven't you been up here to see me? And why you ain't put no money on my books?" I asked.

"Nigga, in case you didn't know, your bitch made sure Tec wasn't giving me shit so what I have, I will be using to live. Fuck, you have free shelter and meals so I don't see why you need money anyway. Look I have to go and tend to Ezra," she said before disconnecting the call. Looking at my phone, I wanted to choke this bitch. This was the third time in two weeks she had hung up on me. It probably would have been more if her dumb ass had been answering my calls. I went to call her back before I was interrupted.

"Guard!" my cellmate warned, causing me to hide my phone just as he rounded the corner.

"What the fuck are you up to, Pierre?" the fat guard asked mugging me. Her ugly fat ass used to forever try to throw ass at me and because I declined she was forever hating.

"Minding my fucking business. What the fuck you want?" I mugged.

"Keep talking to me like you the one in charge and watch you live to regret it nigga. You may have these other guards in your pocket but not me!"

"What do you want with me?" I asked, mugging her ass.

"You have a visitor." To say I was surprised was an understatement. Dynastii hasn't been back since Ashanti walked in on us and to be honest, I was missing my shorty. I walked backwards towards the guard with my hands behind my back so that she could cuff me and take me to the visitation room.

"You sure have a lot of bitches," she said while she led the way. "I met two fiancées and now I'm meeting a girlfriend." Before she could elaborate, another guard walked up.

"I got him, the warden needs you," he told her. The walk over was quiet until I noticed him taking me to a room that was hardly used because it was further from the rest.

"Why are we going back here?" I asked now alert.

"Don't question me, I told you to walk so fucking walk," he answered, shoving me forward. Walking in my eyes landed on some white chick with blonde hair.

"I think you have me in the wrong room." I looked at the guard who shook his head, uncuffed me, and walked away.

"Nah, you're right where you need to be. I would ask how you are but seeing where you are answers that question." She smirked standing to her feet. Lil' mama was slim fine and on second look, you could tell she was mixed with something.

"Yo, who the fuck are you?" I asked not wanting to beat around the bush. I was already pissed off cause I thought I would be seeing Dynastii.

"I'm Chloe but you can call me your life saver. Have a seat we don't have much time." She motioned towards the bench.

"I don't know you, shorty. I'll stand. What's good?" I declined the seat.

"Look I'm here to help you but if you want to act like a bitch I can definitely bounce. It's your life on the line." She answered standing to walk out the door. My eyes looked at her toned legs and swept up the length of them until her dress halted my visual assault.

"How the fuck you get in here with that short dress?" I asked, licking my lips.

My dick started getting hard and I knew I needed to calm down. If it was one thing I knew it was money, and this bitch was dripping it. I wish her ass was Dynastii because I know she would let me hit it since we were way back here. You could hear the guards coming at least a minute before they got here if they were casually making rounds. It had been months since Ashanti came through and hit me with a quickie so a nigga had to resort to beating his dick in the dark. It was straight for what it was but nothing could compete with sliding in something wet and warm.

"I guess since Ashanti and Dynastii quit your ass you ain't been getting no pussy, huh?" she asked, reading my mind and licking her full lips. Those bitches had to be surgically done or she damn sure wasn't white. I had never seen a white chick with lips this big, naturally. Her skin looked the color of honey but then again that could be a tan.

"That ain't none of your business. Fuck them bitches. When I get out of this motherfucker, them hoes getting taken care of!" I snapped, feeling myself getting mad again. I took care of both of these hoes and they left me hanging.

"That's if you get out. The information I have could have your ass dying in the shower," she replied, walking towards me.

"What information?"

"That depends, what are you going to do for me?" she asked dragging a finger up the length of my dick. Slapping her hand, I took a step back. I watched as a smile spread across her lips. "Look I know what happened with Ahmad and you know what's going to happen if Tec finds out what happened with Ahmad. I'm the only thing stopping you from dying in prison." I felt like my body went in shock from what she was saying. No one was supposed to know I had anything to do with that bullshit. Tec could play that, I ain't in the game role, but his ass was more ruthless than Ahmad was. I was in deep thought until I felt her warm mouth wrap around my dick. I didn't even feel when she pulled my pants down.

"Sssss fuckkkk!" I moaned like a bitch as I grabbed the back of her head and guided her down on my dick. Normally I was a no hands type of nigga but the fact the she had my dick in her mouth but was gripping the shit out of the rest had a nigga eyes crossing. Making a loud popping noise, she removed my dick and begin licking on my balls before putting them in her mouth. "Fucking right," I said when she didn't miss a beat and started beating my dick while snaking her tongue around my balls. I tried to think about dogs and cats and shit so I wouldn't bust, but she fucked that idea up.

"Nah daddy, stop holding back. Get this one out the way so you can deep stroke this pussy," she said before shoving my dick back down her throat. Without my permission nut started shooting from my dick to the back of her throat. I knew I was in for some freak shit when she gargled my nut then swallowed it. A nigga had to catch his breath as she took off her dress and stood in front of me in just a thong. Her titties were sitting pretty as a motherfucker and my mouth instantly began to water. The size of them mixed with piercings in them had me thinking of Dynastii and I wanted to kill the bitch and fuck her at the same time.

"How long we got?" I asked, stroking my throbbing dick.

"I paid them to leave us alone for an hour. You wasted a good fifteen minutes and we still haven't talked," she said, turning around so her back was facing me. I watched as she bent all the way over and slid the thong down her legs.

"So fucking talk," I said and with no warning I grabbed her by the waist and stuffed my dick in her tight, wet pussy. A nigga felt like he was in the twilight zone sliding in her. There was an instant tingle in the back of my legs.

"Oooohhhh fuck take your time, Preeeezzzzzzz!" She moaned as a started stroking.

I knew it had been a while since she got some dick cause her pussy was chocking the fuck out of me. I slapped her hand away as she tried to slow down my strokes. I had a lot of pent up aggression and hadn't had pussy in too fucking long. My bitches up and left me and Dynastii had the nerve to move on with a nigga like I hadn't been holding her down. Yeah, Chloe's ass was about to feel this pressure.

"Nah bitch, you came here for dick, huh. So. That's. What. The. Fuck. You're. Getting," I said, digging deeper with every word. The bitch had this look of shock on her face the whole time. I felt like I had fucked the voice out of her. Her eyes told me she wanted to say something but it was stuck in her throat. Removing my dick and backing up I watched her limp body fall to the floor. The juices were leaking from her pussy and my dick was shiny from how wet her shit was.

"Preeezzzzz, why you stopped?" she whined getting up from the floor.

"Shit, because I ain't fucking no corpse shawty. You better

earn this dick, fuck it back, and I said start talking. If you want this dick stop all that fucking screaming and tell me why you here," I said, grabbing a handful of her hair and throwing her towards the chair she was sitting on. I could tell she liked this rough shit and that's all the fuck I was offering.

"Grab the legs of the chair!" I demanded. *WHAP!* Her ass immediately turned red under the strength of my slap. "Yo ass don't fucking listen. I didn't say the seat of it. Grab the legs so I can go balls deep."

After she fixed herself, I mercilessly shoved my dick back in her already swollen pussy. *WHAP!*

"Oooohhhh Prez I-I ammmm gra-grabbing the chaaiiiiirr-rrr." She could barely get her words out as I hit her ass with death strokes.

"I said talk!" I growled trying to think about everything but how juicy this pussy was.

"A-A-shanti wwaasss my... Oh Fuck! My friend," she said, throwing her pussy back on my dick. "Shhheee's going tell T-tec that you killed his brother so he'll f-f-fuck with her- ooooh shiiiitttt- again," she said, making me go deeper than I intended. Pulling out I looked at that bitch like she lost her mind.

"Ashanti wouldn't do no shit like that!" I said, refusing to believe her.

"You don't know the bitch like you think you do," she said, climbing on top of the table and spreading her legs so I could see the prettiest pussy. That shit made my unintentionally lick my lips but I wasn't eating no foreign pussy. "You damn near about to drool daddy, come eat my pussy then shove that dick back in me."

"Shorty, I don't eat random bitch's pussy," I told her honestly.

"I'm saving your life. Nigga, eat my pussy or get the fuck out and I can make the guard finish up," she told me dead ass serious.

"You told me what I needed to know so shit, call him." I shrugged.

"Nigga, I still haven't told you how to save your life or the other shit." She smirked. I wanted to act like I didn't care but a nigga was interested as fuck.

"What other shit?"

"I know your biggest secret." The look of confusion that spread across her face caused her to continue. "Shit that would make Dynastii turn into a bigger problem than Tec. Shit that would make her skin your ass alive." She paused and a smile spread across her face. "I can tell by the way your eyes bulged that you know exactly what I'm talking about. You wasting time so don't even worry about the head, just come finish me off, unless, you ready to live your last days."

My dick jumped at the way she was talking. This bitch knew what she wanted and had some of the best pussy I had ever run in. Pulling her to the edge of the table, I slid my dick back inside of her and didn't stop until I was balls deep. I grabbed her by the neck and pulled her even more closer.

"Let me find out you on some snake shit and your ass goin' be living in your last days," I harshly whispered in her ear before punishing her pussy. Every time I thrust deeper in her, I pulled her body down towards mine. Squeezing her neck tighter, I watched her eyes roll to the back of her head and she started squirting all over as I decorated her walls with my kids. I pulled out of her and the bitch was still squirting.

"Damn. Your secret is safe with me. Look me up, when you get out," she said, hopping down, slipping on her thong, and throwing her dress over her head.

"Nah bitch, how the fuck I'm supposed to stay alive?"

"Sorry you had to hear it from me but your ex is in love with Tec. Tell Dynastii that it was Ashanti who killed Ahmad.

And tell her why, make it good so you aren't included in the bullshit. She may kill your ass behind him if you are mixed in. All you have to do is plant the seed. That bitch is bad; she'll make sure the garden blossoms," she said, placing a kiss on my lips then walking out like she hadn't just fucked up my head.

The guard walked in just as I was fixing my clothes to take me back to my cell. As I laid in my bunk, I thought of what I would tell Dynastii tomorrow when I got her to come here.

Chapter 20:

Dynastii

"I'm going fuck Sage's white ass up!" Mizanii said, walking in my house without knocking as usual.

"What he do now?" I mumbled as I tried to reach Amir for the what felt like the hundredth time today. When I woke up this morning, he was already gone and a couple of hours had gone by without as much as a text.

"Look at this shit!" she said, shoving her phone in my face. I looked at the picture for a while then read the words underneath it before I felt the tears welling up in my eyes and crying with laughter.

"Bitch I know he didn't! This nigga is out of line." I laughed.

"That's just it though, he ain't no fucking nigga bruh. This white boy has entirely too much balls," she said, looking pissed.

"And apparently dick too. Y'all were loud as fuck yesterday," Serenity said, walking in with Amor directly behind her laughing, "Anyway, I didn't know you decided to permanently stay with Sage, Mizanii," she said, causing me to fall out laughing again.

"Bitch, because I didn't tell his ass I was staying there. Something is seriously wrong with his ass. And he's under the picture taking bids, look," she said, going back to her Facebook page.

"Dynastii, let me see your phone?" Z asked before snatching it and dialing a number.

"Who is she calling?" Amor asked, causing me to shrug.

"Oh, but you're going answer Dynastii's call, huh? Sage, I'm convinced you really are a crack baby, nigga is you crazy? Take that shit off my Facebook and change my password back NOW!" she said, causing me to laugh even louder. "You're taking bids to sell my house though, bruh? And starting at twenty punk ass dollars. Sage, where are you?" she asked as Amor and Serenity joined in on the laughter.

"Mizanii, stop tripping that shit is funny," I said further pissing her off.

"No, the fuck it ain't. Dynastii shut up talking to me, y'all in here like a nigga playing with him. I love my house." She stomped in place before looking at the screen of my phone then placing it back to her ear.

"Aye, let me holla at Sage right quick." Without waiting on a reply, I snatched the phone. "Hello," I said, grabbing his attention.

"Yo, Wassup D- Nastii, why is your girl over there tripping on me man. I'm just trying to make sure my wife stays right where the fuck she belongs," he said, laughing.

"Y'all have problems. But on some real shit, you heard from your boy today?" I asked about Amir.

"Not since last night when y'all was together. Today would have been Ahmad's birthday so you know how that goes," he said, causing me to nod in understanding.

"Oh ok, I had no idea. The least he could do is answer and let me know he's ok. Sage, Z's goin' hit you later someone is calling my phone private," I said, looking at the screen.

"Oh yeah they been calling," Mizanii answered nonchalantly causing me to roll my eyes.

"Z, that could have been Amir!" I snapped, answering the phone before they hung up. "Hello?"

"Dynastii, don't hang up please! It's important." Hearing Prez's voice immediately put a bad taste in my mouth.

"Nigga, you must have dialed the wrong number. What the fuck do you want, President?" I asked, causing Amor, Mizanii and Serenity to stop what they were doing and direct their attention my way.

"I need to talk to you, please Dy. It's life or death," he damn near begged causing me to roll my eyes.

"We don't have anything to talk about Prez. My man wouldn't appreciate me on the phone with you. Unlike some people, I don't cheat. So, you have a good life," I said, removing the phone from my ear until I heard him scream.

"It's about Tec!"

"What about him?" I asked as I placed the phone back on my ear.

"I tell you it's life or death and you don't care but as soon as I say it's about him you're all ears huh? Damn Dynastii that's fucked up, ma," he said, sounding like I hurt him to the core.

"What do you have to tell me about my man, Prez?" I asked feeling myself lose patience with him.

"That's what we on," he chuckled. "Be at my visitation today. Dynastii if you don't show up that's on you, but Tec goin' suffer," he said, hanging up in my ear. Looking at my watch, I saw I had a few hours before visitation so I jumped up and headed for the shower.

"Uh, uh where the fuck are you going?" Mizanii asked, following me.

"To see Prez," I answered, walking to my closet and pulling out some clothes.

"Oh, you bitch's really bad, Amir goin' fuck your ass up and then kill Prez. Just wait on it, my brother ain't all there. You get the calm Tec and think shit sweet." Amor laughed as she walked back in my room eating a donut.

"He said it has something to do with Amir, I need to know what's going on," I said as I shimmied into the light wash denim skinny jeans. I threw on a white V-neck t-shirt and tied a red, blue, and white plaid shirt around my waist. Throwing on a pair of red chucks, I noticed no one was talking but they were all looking at me.

"What the fuck is the problem?" I snapped.

"You sure you going cause it's about Amir or is it because you really want to see Prez? Let's keep it real, y'all go through this cycle all the time. The difference this time is you have a good man in your corner now, Dynastii," Mizanii said, pissing me off.

"And I could remember telling you I'm going because he said it has something to do with that good man you're speaking of. It's been literally months since I have spoken to Prez so don't act like this is some sneaky ass mission I'm on. Lock my damn house on y'all way out," I said before Mizanii made me go off on her ass.

Hitting the highway, I did the dash until I was at the prison. I said I wasn't making this drive anymore but look what the fuck love had me doing, my love for Amir anyway. Going through the motions of getting check in my mind drifted back to where Amir could be. I was so into my thoughts, I didn't see Prez walk in until he threw his arms around me.

"Uh, uh nigga, back up," I said, mushing his forehead. The look of shock on his face almost made me laugh.

"What, that nigga won't let you hug an old friend?" he asked, letting out an angry laugh.

"Prez, you know no one tells me what to do. I won't hug your ass because I'm loyal. Some shit you know nothing about. So, what is so important I had to make the drive way out here?" I asked, cutting to the chase. Instead of answering, he decided to take a seat and stare me down.

"You used to make the drive with no complaints," he replied.

"Yep, when I thought I had a loyal nigga. But since you ain't, the fuck you want Prez?"

"You're looking good, Dynastii, getting thick and shit. Is that nigga treating you better than I was?" he asked.

"Let me see, he's supportive, loving, kind, wants better for me than I want for myself, doesn't cheat and didn't have a secret baby. Shit, I would say that he does." I shrugged.

"Man shit just happened with that bitch; she wasn't supposed to have no baby by me. Fuck, I ain't ready for kids," he said, making me mug his ass.

"Bitch then learn how to fucking wrap up cause as far as I know your ass had two already. Prez, stop playing with me. I ain't here to talk about you or that bitch, Ashanti. I'm here to talk about Tec."

"Well then that means you did come to talk about all of us. This is about Ashanti ass too," he said, grabbing my attention. "Look how much do you know about Tec?" he asked.

"I know enough, why?" I replied rolling my eyes.

"So, you know about his brother Ahmad?" he asked.

"Yeah, I do, but I don't understand what he has to do with Ashanti. She was Tec's ex not Ahmad's." I replied.

"Her being Tec's *fiancée* didn't stop her from fucking Ahmad any chance she got. So, don't say that like it means something."

"Her being Tec's fiancée didn't stop you from fucking her either I see," I said, showing that I was still a lil' bitter.

"Look I called you here because she's trying to set me up."

"In what way, I'm confused." Stepping closer to me, I

flinched as he brought his lips to my ear. .

"I'm in here for killing Ahmad's homeboy. I didn't kill him though; she did and is going to throw it on me," he whispered.

"What the fuck? What beef did you have with his homeboy? Nigga, I asked who you were beefing with!" I snapped. "And why would she even bring this back up if the streets aren't talking about this?"

"Look I can't get into all that. All I know is she feels that telling Tec what he needs to hear will make him give her a second chance, despite him being with you. I think she's setting Tec up though. She pillow talked often, she wants his money but him gone."

"What made you tell me this?" I asked not understanding what he had to gain.

"I guess I'm being selfish. I know that you will do whatever to protect those you love. You're pissed off with me but there is still love there for sure. And as much as I feel like you left a nigga hanging, I know you love him too. You're goin' have to get rid of her ass to keep him and me alive. If she starts talking, he's goin' send someone at my head and she just goin kill him once she gets the money." He shrugged as I put my head in my hands. Killing someone was old news to me but this shit was too much drama.

"Prez, after I handle this, don't reach out to me anymore. Where does she stay?" I asked. I watched as panic set in his face.

"Nah, you can't do that shit at her house. My son is there. Catch her when she's out somewhere," he said as the guard walked in. I stared him down as he was cuffed and removed. This nigga had the nerve to ignore my son but was falling in head first for hers. Fuck what he heard; I was going to her house, tonight! She was the reason I lost one man, that's wouldn't happen again.

***

After facing two blunts the smoke in the car was thick as I

tried to wrap my head around what was going on.

"Maybe it's not what it seems," Z said, looking at me through compassion filled eyes. The choice to pick her and Serenity up on my way here was a no brainer, but as I sat here, I started to regret it. I didn't need compassion, I wanted the anger to take over.

"It seems like my nigga been ignoring my ass and when I pull up to his ex bitch house his truck parked like he lives here. That ain't what it seems to y'all? I asked laughing to stop the angry tears from falling.

"Anything could have happened, let's not jump to conclusions." Serenity said as I mashed the blunt in the ashtray and stepped out of the car. I hear their doors close behind me.

"How are we going in?" Mizanii asked as Serenity simply turned the doorknob on the front door and it opened. "How did you know it was unlocked?" Mizanii asked her.

"Boujie hoes never lock their doors," Serenity answered as we entered the house and pulled our guns out.

"Z, her son is in here." I said pointing to the bedroom with dinosaurs on the door. "We'll drop his ass at a church or something. Make sure you grab him. Serenity you see if someone is in there. Check restrooms too." There were three bedrooms so we all took a room. Twisting the doorknob, I felt my heart beating out of my chest as my eyes landed on a sleeping Amir lying next to Ashanti. As if she felt me in her bedroom Ashanti popped up and looked around until her eyes landed on me. A smirk graced her face until I cocked my gun.

"Nah hoe, smile again I dare you," I said.

"Where's my baby, Dynastii?" she asked

"I don't touch kids, he's good. He's about to be motherless, but he's good," I answered. Hearing my voice, a groggy Amir woke up.

"Ashanti... Dynastii... The fuck is going on?" he asked, faking confusion. I tried hard to stop the tears from falling, but this shit hurt me to my core. Pulling out my second gun, I sat deciding if I should even tell him what Ashanti did. Maybe I should let the bitch ruin p

him.

"Don't insult my intelligence Amir! Let me tell you what kind of bitch you're laid up with—"

"DYNASTII! COME HERE QUICK!" I heard Mizanii scream damn near in tears causing me to run full speed out the room. Walking into the baby's room, I got the shock of my life.

"No, no it can't be. Is that... Is that Malakhi?"

Chapter 21:

Chloe

I watched as Ashanti blew my phone up for what had to have been the twelfth time and simply rolled my eyes. Any moment now a text would be coming through from her ass and that too would go ignored. It had been over two months since she hysterically called me crying because she had to leave the state and her funds are running low. I don't know why she felt like calling me would be the thing to do but she did. I listened to her cry while I shed tears of my own. Tears of joy that is. I simply had the phone on mute while I celebrated her downfall. This is what I was waiting for, her life to crumble around her. The audacity of her to expect from me, what she could not be. For her to think I was a true friend was nuts and baffled me. Like clockwork, my phone alert me of an incoming text message. Rolling my eyes, I ignored the fact that my nails may still be slightly wet and unlocked it.

Ashanti: Chloe, I need to talk. I'm losing it!

I laughed as I read the message then threw my phone onto the bed. Walking out of the empty master bedroom, I made my way down the hall. Gabbing the face mask, gloves and air freshener that sat outside the door, I walked in while spraying an ample amount and adjusting the mask on my face. The room smelled like old piss and shit and nearly made me vomit. Even the mask and strong air freshener couldn't help to cover this stench. I almost felt bad. **Almost.**

"Father, you really[PA5] stink." I called out as his eyes followed me into the room. The frail man sitting up in the chair in the corner of the room was a fraction of my first love and heart-break. I couldn't help but to shake my head at what he drove me to do. He made me hold him hostage. He made me show a side of myself that I would have never exposed him to. When my mother killed herself, the only thing she left behind was a fucking five-word note: *Your father is to blame!* That's it, that's all I got. He didn't even help me bury her either. Meanwhile, Ashanti had a new Benz from her secret boo. Too bad for her, the cat was out of the bag. She had to pay for what she did to my family but I couldn't blame only her. My father was the adult here so clearly, he was just as responsible as she was. All I wanted was his love but he couldn't give it to me. He was too busy giving it to her ass. How could some loose pussy hoe shake the bond that we had happily formed from the moment of my birth. What type of power did she have over him? I felt the tears in my eyes and forced them back, I was hurt but he would never see it. Walking over, I ripped the tape from his mouth and watched as his lips slightly bled from being so dry.

"Chloe... please?" He begged as usual and just like any other time, I laughed at his ass.

"Chloe please, what?" I asked laughing at his expense. "Huh, father? Chloe please what? You are so lucky I am in a great mood today. I ordered you some food and I'm even going to allow you to wash your ass and clean your room." I said with a smile. "Get up!" I said raising my voice and causing him to jump a little. It so crazy how my tiny ass had him terrified. I grabbed the scissors to cut the tape from his legs and arms and passed the walker that sat in the corner over to him. His next words stopped me from freeing him though.

"Chloe... I'm your father. You have to let me go." He whispered. He was too weak to even complete a sentence and that was just how I wanted it. Grabbing the roll of tape, I placed it on his lips. Before I could reply to that bullshit he had just spat, I heard knocking from the door letting me know that his food had arrived.

"Don't make a sound." I spat before walking away. Removing the gloves and mask, I fixed my clothing then made my way to the front door.

"This damn house looks abandoned." I heard on the other side of the door.

"Oh, it's very much occupied." I replied swinging it open. I rolled my eyes as the delivery man hungrily took in my appearance. I was used to it but I was annoyed by the situation I had to handle.

"He-hello. Delivery for Ashanti." He finally said still staring in awe.

"Yep, that's me. Here you go." I replied tipping him and accepting the meal from Olive Garden. It smelled amazing but this meal was strictly for my father. I gave the name Ashanti because I wanted everything to fall back on her ass once my plan was over and done with. When I noticed he hadn't made a move to leave I couldn't help the smirk that instantly graced my face. Growing up, I was always the last bitch to get chose. We stayed in the hoods where the men wanted those beautiful black chicks with the round asses and hips that wouldn't quit. Even I stared down their round lips and the way they filled out the stylish clothing that I secretly admired. A poor looking white girl in the hood with no hips, ass, lips or style did nothing for them. My father finally came in handy when I snatched his ass up because his job as an attorney gave me access to a lovely bank account. With the swipe of a card, I became the very female that I admired. Well at least a good knock off, anyway. I paid for so many surgeries that I can't even keep count of and became the woman I always wanted to be. My ass was fat, hips were poking, titties were sitting up like a baby's ass on my chest and my lips were defined and full. I tanned my ass off and colored my hair blonde so that I looked a lil exotic. Despite the daily catcalls, the dates and the men I fucked, I never got enough of the attention. I lived for that shit.

"How old are you?" I asked as I placed the food on the counter top.

"Se-seventeen." He nervously replied as I slowly walked back over to him. He was fine as fuck but I could tell having a grown woman approach him knocked him off his square. Hell, I was about to allow him to live out every delivery boy's dream. He was about to get fucked something proper.

"What's your name?" I asked standing in front of him with my hands on my hips and my legs slightly spread apart.

"Zay- Zayvion." He answered licking his lips ass he eyes trailed the length of my body before settling on my full, man-made breast. Walking closer, I made sure they were so close to his face if he stuck his tongue out he would taste them.

"That's cute. Zayvion." I repeated his name letting it roll off my tongue. I reached one of my pointy fingernails out and traced his dick that was damn near pitching a tent in his pants. Giving it a firm squeeze, I was pleasantly surprised that Zayvion may have been a teenager but his dick was a grown ass man. "Can I call you Zay?" I asked pressing my breast against his chest as I leaned forward and licked his ear. I heard him gasp and could damn near bet every single penny in my account that homeboy almost nut on himself.

"I- I gotta go back..." he started before I interrupted him.

"Zay, you don't gotta do nothing but shove your big black dick in my wet pussy!" I replied grabbing his hand and allowing it to rub against my freshly shaved pussy. I was wearing a fitted red tank dress with absolutely nothing underneath it so his fingers were able to glide along my wetness. "Breathe baby breathe." I teased because poor baby was about to fuck around and die real quick.

"I have... I have a girl." He forced himself to say but he never snatched his hand away. In fact, his fingers were roaming on their own.

"Is she here?" I questioned.

"No ma'am." He quickly answered.

"So why the fuck would you bring her up? I have a man but since he ain't here, I want your dick." I halfway lied. Shit if my plans went like I know they better go, I was about to save Prez's life and we would run off together. Serving Ashanti her final fuck you and making sure I got my happily ever after all in one. "Have y'all fucked before?" I questioned.

"Huh?" I rolled my eyes at him being so naïve. It had been weeks since I fucked Prez and I needed some dick in the worse way. Thing was, I didn't want just any kind of dick! I needed this boy to fuck me until I was walking crazy. I needed him to fuck me so good that I momentarily forgot my name. With a dick like his and a pussy like mine this could be magical but if his ass didn't know how to use that shit right, it would only piss me off.

"Nigga, are you a virgin?" I spat getting pissed off. I attempted to control my anger but when I wanted something, I never liked to do too much talking.

"N- No! I had sex a few times." He answered puffing his chest out like I had wounded his ego and he wanted me to show him some respect.

"But do you know how to fuck?" When his chest deflated a bit and a confused look crossed his face I continued. "I can tell you don't know what I mean. When I'm finished with you here today your bitch will need to send me a check in the mail. Get naked!" I demanded.

"What?" He asked with his eyes bulging. I didn't reply as I removed my dress from over my head and stood in front of him in only my Giuseppe sandals. His damn zipper almost broke thanks to his dick growing stronger than Popeye on some spinach. "You sure about this?" He asked nervously looking around.

"Zay, if your lil scared ass don't get undressed the only thing I'm going be sure about is that you more pussy than the one between my legs!" I spat. As if he had something to prove, he placed the money and receipt in his pocket and unfastened his belt. I licked my lips as his pants fell to the floor exposing his thick and meaty dick. Baby, I don't know what they were feeding these children but they were creating porn stars in the making. Spinning around, I walked away from him making sure I added an extra bounce with every step. I knew my ass was bouncing like a basketball in the hands of Kobe. When I looked over my shoulder, he was removing his shoes so that his legs could be free of his jeans and boxers. Sitting atop the dining room table, I spread my legs and motioned for him to come closer. His dick lead the way and as soon as he was in arms reach, I grabbed him by the collar of his uniform shirt and pulled him closer.

"Fuccccckkk." He moaned out when his dick rubbed against my wet folds. Nervously, he attempted to back away but I quickly wrapped my legs around him and pulled in closer. My eyes rolled to the back of my head when his dick pressed slightly into my pussy. Grabbing his neck, I brought his lips to mine and to my surprise his lil ass kissed me with the passion grown men couldn't imitate. I don't even know what made me kiss him because my only goal was a nut but I was surely glad that I did. I didn't want it to end and from the way he was moaning, he didn't either. Hungrily, I sucked on his tongue and like it gave him a boost of confidence, his hands gripped my breast like he paid for those bitches. Breaking the kiss, I smirked at the look on his face. He hadn't even smelled my pussy yet he was in love.

"Open your mouth and stick your tongue out." I whispered and like he was under some sort of spell, he complied. Rubbing my nipple along his tongue, my body shuddered. "You know what to do or do I need to guide you?" I asked raising an eyebrow. Instead of answering, he hungrily popped one of my breast into his mouth as he groped the other one. I threw my head back in ecstasy as he made love to each one of my breast with just his mouth. I was too far gone when I felt his fingers into my pussy and he began to move them in a come here motion.

As I lifted my head to moan out I was stopped when his mouth covered mine and he shoved his tongue into my open mouth. I think I had the wrong idea about lil baby. He may have been timid when I was speaking to him but something told me his dick game was about to be proper. When he pulled his fingers from my pussy and forced them in my mouth, I knew then that I was in for a ride. Ain't no way his ass was new to knocking down walls. As I sucked on his fingers, I was unaware that he was about to take my fucking breath away. Literally. Without warning, Zay shoved his dick into my wet pussy.

"Fuck man fuck!" He said as my walls squeezed his dick for dear life. I couldn't catch my breath and damn sure couldn't speak as his big dick felt like it was knocking my walls down. After a little maneuvering, he was in as far as he could go without nutting, yet he still wasn't all the way in. "Damn, this pussy tight." He said wiping his forehead then gripping my hips like they were going to disappear. After he placed a quick kiss on my lips, he went in for the kill. Zay started fucking my pussy like he had a point to prove and trust me, he was proving it.

"Oooohhhh fuuuucccckkk Zay! Fuucckkk me!" I screamed out grinding my hips to match his thrust.

"You like that shit?" He surprised me by talking shit back. "Huh, you like how I'm fucking you?" He asked digging deeper. I wanted to answer but he was fucking me senseless and I was still shocked that this was the same dude that was stuttering. "You can't talk now, you wanted some black dick and now you can't handle it." He said slamming into me and causing me to start squirting. I don't know if it was his stroke game or his mouth piece but he had me forgetting he was seventeen. Pulling out of me, he placed his mouth on my pussy and made a loud slurping sound as he sucked my pussy like a Slurpee. As he got full off of my juices, I heard noises coming from the back of the house and knew my father was up to something. Leave it so him to ruin shit for me. I also knew he was too weak to really move fast so I was going to finish up here before I went deal with his ass. Pushing Zay back, I jumped up on my heels and bent forward over the table so that he could hit it from the back. There wasn't a man alive that could last long once I let him slide in during this position. Reaching back with my left hand, I grabbed his dick and pulled him closer to me. Rubbing his dick against my wet slit, I moaned in ecstasy.

"Shiiittttt." He called out while biting his lip. I guided his dick into my awaiting pussy and allowed my pussy walls to once again suck him in until he was balls deep. I adjusted to his size before I started throwing it back faster than he could handle it. I knew I was separating the boys from the men when I did this shit. I was a pro at fucking and he was a boy playing in a woman's pussy at this point. I know I could slow up and let him catch his breath but I had better shit to do. The sound of my ass clapping on his dick threw me into overdrive. If I wasn't on a mission to get my man Prez, I may have actually snatched his lil ass up and taught him a few things. His bitch should thank me because I'm definitely doing her young ass a favor. In between the sounds of my ass giving me a standing ovation and him moaning out like a bitch, I heard my father attempting to scream out against the tap and obviously he did too.

"I... oh shit! I hear... Oooohhhh fuck! Something in the-the back. Fuck this pussy good!" He attempted to form a complete sentence but my pussy had his dick in a chokehold and my juices were dripping down to his balls.

"It's a dog." I responded reaching back and spreading my ass cheeks so he could go deeper. "Fuck me, Zay. Fuck me hard! Grab my hair!" I called out. Again, my wish was his command. Releasing my hips, he not only grabbed a fistful of my hair but he got so close that I could no longer throw it back how I wanted to. Placing his hand firmly around my neck, he was in full control as he chocked me and started delivering some death strokes. I could do nothing but slightly lift my leg to give him better access. With his mouth to my ear. He began talking shit again.

"Damn, this some good pussy!" He moaned out before slamming his dick into me relentlessly. "You a pretty bitch with some bomb ass pussy!" He said before pulling my head back by my hair and sucking my lips in. Releasing my hair and my lips, he placed both hands around my neck and started savagely fucking me. I loved this shit but I was sure I would need a new pussy after this was all said and done.

"FUCK. ME. HARDER. I'M. ABOUT. TO. CUM!" I screamed out in between his deep strokes. I could barely breathe but I didn't give a fuck.

"Shit me too!" He called out as he released his seeds in me at the same time that I began nutting. I fell against the table as he fell onto my back and continued with a few more subtle pumps fully releasing his seeds. "Fuck, that shit was bomb!" He said damn near out of breath. I couldn't speak yet but I knew I wasn't done with him.

"What time do you have to be back to work, I need to take a ride on that." I said referring to his dick.

"If I don't answer, they just assume I don't want to pick up that order." He shrugged looking excited.

"Get you a water out the refrigerator. I'm going check on my dog, he'll be lucky if I don't kill his ass." I shot a wicked smirk over my shoulder before throwing my ass back so he knew it was time for him to get up. "Do whatever you have to do to make sure when I get back, your dick is at attention." I said before walking off. I didn't even throw on any clothes, just grabbed the bag of food and headed to the unoccupied room of the house. Digging in the closet, I grabbed the already grounded up rat poison I had been feeding my father and put way more than normal into the pasta I ordered him. I mixed it so that it blended with the alfredo sauce and smiled because after he did me one more favor, that was it for him. Slipping a robe on, I made my way to his room where he succeeded into falling on the floor. I grabbed the gloves and face mask again before sitting his stinking ass up on the chair and ripping the tape from his mouth.

"Chloe... Please!" He begged again like his extensive vocabulary had failed him. Those were the only words he ever said. He should know I was too far gone to act like shit would be okay if I just freed him.

"Shut up. Listen to me and listen to me well, I have one more favor to ask of you then I will let you run back to that bitch Ashanti. Here is your food, eat! When I come back you will do a favor for me and then you are free to go. I trust you will keep your mouth shut about this, right daddy? You owe it to me. You are the reason mom killed herself!" I spat. His eyes even lit up like he actually believed me and he nodded his head up and down. "I have company so one word and you will die!" I warned him as he again nodded. "Good, eat!" I said as he ate the only way I allowed him to. He put his face in the plate like a dog would. Call me crazy all you want to, he ruined my life so I ruined his before I would end his shit. I had no time to dwell on him, I needed a final ride before I went pick my man up!

Chapter 22:

Mizanii

Swinging the door opened I shook my head at Amor and Serenity as they walked in holding hands. They were really cute together and I loved when they matched each other's swag. Like right now they were both rocking a pair of fitted, distressed, light wash skinny leg jeans with a pair of nude peep toe red bottoms. Their shirt though the same was different. It was a graphic Dare shirt but Amor's shirt was cut as a crop top and Serenity's shirt was sleeveless and exposed a shit load of side boob. Even their hairstyles were alike. Amore had an asymmetrical bob with a middle part and Serenity's once long hair was also in a bob with a deep side part. Some people would think this was weird but I thought it was real cute.

"Why you shaking you forever shaking your head at us?" Serenity asked knowing why. No, it is not what you are thinking. Serenity and I fucked whenever I wanted to walk on that side of the street but I didn't want her like that. Pussy couldn't keep me happy until the end of my days. I ain't like no pussy that much besides my own, get me?

"Cause, Aunt B goin fuck y'all up and I want no parts in that shit. Y'all need to tell her crazy asses that y'all together and get it over with." I replied closing the door behind them as they walked in.

"You see how she reacted when you told her you and Sage got married because y'all was drunk? Then you almost killed her when you told her you was trying to get that shit annulled. Her ass wants to be a Christian when she feels like being one. She fine when she is cursing up a storm though." Amor said rolling her eyes. I couldn't help but to laugh because between Sage, Tec and Aunt B asses they treated her like a baby. She had a point though, I thought Aunt B was going fuck me up because I wanted to divorce "her baby", as she called him. She lectured for hours about how marriage was everlasting and she could see the love we shared for each other. I think her ass needed glasses. Sage made my ass itch. Walking to the kitchen, I grabbed them both a bottle of water and a banana for myself before joining them on the ugly ass sectional Sage had picked out. I hated it from the bottom of my foundation but he seemed to think the shit was cute for some reason. I don't think it was ugly, it just wasn't mine. I was still Louisiana summer hot that his ass sold my fucking home and forced me to move here.

"Why you all frowned up?" Serenity asked.

"Girl I'm tired of being here! I want my own fucking house back." I whined and stumped my feet like a big ass child.

"I thought you were going to give this all a chance? I love y'all together, despite how y'all ended up married. I see how serious he is with you? I never saw him take a female serious before you and I can really tell that he loves you. You really don't feel anything for Sage?" Amore asked. I side eyed her ass because she was going to school for family and child psychology and was always trying to make someone a damn test subject. I peeled my banana and took a bite to buy myself some time to think. I obviously took longer than I thought I did because Serenity started laughing her ass off.

"What's funny?" I asked grilling her.

"Cause, you love his ass too. I know you Z! Your ass is in love and trying to deny that shit." She called out still laughing.

"Get out my house!" I said pointing to the door.

"Umm, this Sage house too. I'm in his half." She laughed as my phone began ringing. As soon as I stood up to grab it the call was disconnected and I knew who it was.

"Amor your ass better not tell Tec but Dynastii about to call back." I said shocking their asses. Everyone speculated that I knew where Dynastii was ducked off at but I never confirmed or denied that suspicion.

"You got that from a missed call?" Serenity asked raising a perfectly arched brow.

"She calls from an untraceable number and hangs up before I can answer. That's my cue to make sure I am either by myself or to turn off my phone letting her know that I can't get away to speak. Just wait." I said just as my phone started ringing again. I quickly answered. "Tec or Sage aren't around me. How are you? How is my nephew?" I asked as tears fell down my face. I missed her so damn much. You would have sworn it had been years instead of almost two months since I last saw her. On top of that, I was still in shock that we had actually found my nephew alive and well. The story was one straight out of an urban book and we still didn't know all parties that were involved. Which is why I called in a huge favor. I went behind Serenity's back and got in contact with her very dangerous and very powerful father. He pulled some strings and got my sister and my nephew out of the country for a while. I would eventually tell Serenity but for now I would let sleeping dogs lie. Besides, their drama was another story of its own.

"I'm goin need you to stop all that crying sis." Dynastii said laughing through the phone. "I'm good, Malakhi is good. Everything is good." She said and I heard the happiness in her voice. "My God, he is so damn smart Z! I can't believe I have a second chance at this. I'm still in shock!" she said.

"I know, I know. When will y'all come back. You know Tec is worried about you. That man is going crazy without your ass." I laughed.

"Soon. We will be back real soon. As for Tec, I'm done with his ass. I have some information for him and then that's a rap."

She responded sounding pissed off.

"You haven't even heard his side of the story Dynastii." I said rolling my eyes at her stubbornness.

"My man was in the bed with his ex that kidnapped my child. Z, Tec is lucky he doesn't catch a bullet in the forehead. My heart knows he had nothing to do with this but I'm getting some answers. Once I get all the answers I need and I can guarantee my son will be safe, we will be back." She said.

"I have Amor and Serenity here with me." I said because they were all in my face.

"Bitch, Amor just goin tell her fucking brother you spoke to me. Now he really going be in your damn face about my whereabouts." She said sounding annoyed.

"No, the fuck Amor ain't. That's between you two. I'm just happy that you're safe sis." Amore responded with tears in her eyes. She and Dynastii had really developed a bond.

"I miss and love you Dynastii. Get those answers you are looking for then let us know when you need us to come fuck something up." Serenity called out.

"Love y'all too. I have to go. Stay safe and I'll get back with y'all real soon." She said causing me to cry because the call was being ended. Before I could say bye, the call was disconnected. That was the extent of our calls. We couldn't speak about much or for very long because I was sure Tec and Sage would attempt to track her ass. Just as that call was ending my phone rang again and I couldn't help but to roll my eyes.

"What Sage?" I answered. When I didn't hear him talking I went to disconnect the call until I heard some bitch talking. Hushing Amor and Serenity, I strained my ears to listen in on the conversation. White boy had me all types of fucked up. I could barely make out what the female was saying but I heard loud and clear when Sage blew up on her. When he elevated his voice, she elevated hers also and I was listening in on both parts of the argument. Placing the call on speaker phone, I went into my iPhone and traced Sage's iPhone to a hotel not far from here. They had me fucked up. I listened to the argument as I slipped some tennis shoes on my feet and threw a cropped hoodie over the all in one jumpsuit I was lounging around in.

"Where are you going?" Serenity asked.

"Fuck some bitch name Cheyenne up. I don't know why these hoes think I'm regular in the head. I'm a lil bit fucked up and her ass over there pressing my husband for dick that he just told her at least five times got a ring on it. Bitch told him she don't give a fuck about his wife. Shiiiiitttttttt, she better give a fuck about his wife." I rambled on as they followed me out the house and I listened to the conversation. This thirsty bitch was begging him to suck his dick.

"Oh shit, Cheyenne was a lawyer that had his case thrown out. She been wanting Sage but she doesn't want to be seen in public with him." Amor said as we slid in the car. "Run me your phone real quick." She said and without a second thought I handed it to her.

"What the fuck that mean? She don't want to be seen in public with him like he ugly or something?" I asked getting offended.

"Bitch, you sound a lil bit jealous Just a while ago you didn't want that nigga." Serenity's ass just had to point out. I was quiet for a second as I sped out of my yard and jumped on the highway. I thought about my answer before I replied.

"I ain't take this shit serious because I didn't think Sage did. I thought his ass was joking like he jokes about everything else. Something he just said to that Cheyenne bitch got me thinking he really love my ass. I think I love him too but I'm scared that I'm going fuck this up. I feel like I'm in love but I don't know how to love." I confessed what was holding me back from fully giving myself to my husband.

"Damn. Why don't you just enjoy the journey for what it is? Stop thinking about it too much that way whether y'all make it or not you had fun along the way. Sage is pretty damn dope when you give him a chance." Amor said causing me to nod. "Anyway, his phone hung up but I recorded her ass pressing him for dick and threatening to make his case reappear. After we fuck her up we are going threaten her ass with it." Amor said making sense. Now I didn't have to take my ass in there and get arrested when she called the cops. A bitch like her would do anything for discretion so she would play with my man anymore. My man, I liked the sound of that. In that very moment, I decided that I was no longer running from what Sage and I had. I would give it an honest effort starting today. To sit there and listen to him profess his love to another woman about me was enough to melt the coldest hearts.

Chapter 23:

Prez

"That shit wild as fuck!" I said aloud as the news showed that the body of an unidentified man and a teenage boy were found in a hose burnt to a crisp. The neighboring house were in fire also but they were deserted, so no one was hurt. "Some crazy bitch caught them niggas slipping." I shrugged as I made my way back to my cell. After a few sets of push-ups, I heard those loud ass keys the drug dragged along letting me know one of them were approaching. When I saw it was the CO that I hated, I let out a deep sigh. This bitch was always trying me.

"Pierre! Gather your things!" Hearing the correctional officer scream those words shocked me. The only time I had heard those words were when someone was getting their walking papers and a nigga knew that wasn't the case.

"Yo, where am I going?" I asked already knowing that I was about to catch attitude for even asking that question. This bitch stayed with her attitude on ten and her face puckered up like a fucking bulldog.

"You can stay here if you would like but you have made bail. Get your shit and let's go!" She spat. Her ugly ass didn't have to tell me twice. I didn't want shit that was in that cell so I left it behind for my cellmate, including the iPhone. I was going get my money from Ashanti ass and get whatever the fuck I needed once I was free. I quickly brushed my teeth and I was ready to go. My mind should have been on how the fuck did I make bail if I didn't even have one but shit if they made the mistake I didn't want them to figure it out until I was long gone. They would have to come find me and drag me to any court dates. After being processed out, a nigga stepped outside and sniffed the clear air. That shit smelled way better on this side of the gates. Hopping on the inmate bus that would take me to the bus terminal, I finally let my mind start to process things. I knew what Dynastii and I had was over and that was cool because I wasn't feeling how she up and bounced on me no way. If you ask me, her seeing Ashanti at the visitation was just an excuse for her to leave a nigga high and dry. After all I had done for her ass, I deserved to at least know that she was in my mother fucking corner.

Then there was Ashanti, she would never be my first choice because all her ass loved was a dollar. I couldn't have a bitch on my team that would jump ship anytime the next nigga offered her fifty fuckin cents more than I was. Plus, I wasn't trying to be around her son. Like I said before, I wasn't here to be judged. I never wanted a fucking child.

"Damn!" one of the inmates on the bus called out catching everyone's attention. "That bitch bad and is that a Bentley?" Even the correctional officers that rode the bus broke their neck to take a peak. When I noticed who they were staring at, I couldn't help but to grin. I don't know why but this bad ass whit girl was riding for me harder than the bitches I helped come up. Hopping off the bus, as soon as she saw me she ran into my arms and wrapped her legs around me. I didn't know why she was doing all this shit but I felt like a boss knowing I had the bitch all the niggas wanted, again. Holding her up by her ass, I walked us over to her ride and sat her on top of it.

"You don't look happy to see me." She said making the scent of whatever mint she was sucking slap me in the face.

"I don't know why I'm seeing you." I admitted.

"I made my father call in a favor to a few judges before he died." She replied. "I wanted you free so I made it happen. All I ask is that you remain loyal to me. I don't know why but I fell in love with you. I just want you to be open to what the future can hold for us. At the end of the day, I'm the only person you have on your side." She said making me think. I didn't see it hurting anything to see where this went. Her pussy was grade a and she was fine as fuck with money of her own. Sounded like a win-win situation if you asked me.

"Alright ma, I feel you but I have to get some things together before we can make a move towards anything. I have to get my money from Ashanti." I said as she threw the keys to me and headed to the passenger side. Sliding in the car, I noticed the way she was looking at me. "Wassup?" I asked.

"I don't know how to tell you all of what I have to say, just know I got you through whatever." She said making me side eye her as I started the car and pulled off.

"What's good?" I asked since she hadn't started talking yet.

"Ashanti ran through your money then ran off." She said in one breath. My grip on the steering wheel tightened. "But don't worry about it, I got us." She smiled. Her ass was trying too hard and I could see my robbing her ass blind then moving the fuck on. I ain't like white bitches anyway, slavery fucked that up for them.

"I'm going kill that bitch." I spat. "Ok, then I have to spin by my old crib and get some clothes and shit."

"About that… There was a reason Ashanti went ghost. You don't know it yet but Dynastii went to Ashanti's house a while back. She found her son there. I don't know what she knows for sure yet, but you can't show your face. Ashanti told me about your involvement. Whatever new clothes you need, we will get it tomorrow after we land." She said nonchalantly like she didn't just fuck my head up. That shit with Malakhi was supposed to go to the grave with me. Motherfuckers just didn't understand how his birth ruined shit for me. My money slowed up and I lost my ride or die in a sense. Dynastii didn't want to do shit she deemed as illegal because of his lil ass. So yeah, I snatched him up and passed him to Ashanti. I needed her out my face and I needed my rider back. Obviously, that shit backfired.

"Where we are going tomorrow?" I asked.

"I used another of my father's favors. We have a private plane and we are getting the fuck from around here. Too much shit has happened in a short amount of time. But don't worry about nothing. I got you. I can see you already stressing so let me help you." She said pulling out my dick and giving me the sloppiest head I had ever gotten. I couldn't focus on the road so I pulled over to the side and let her work her magic. On God, she sucked the stress out my dick along with the nut.

"Alright, I'll follow your lead. Where are we going tonight?" I asked knowing I had nowhere else to go.

"I got us a room and I already have you a couple of things there. I'm going make tonight real special for you." She said as she spread her legs and played with her pussy while I drove. Sliding my fingers in her wet pussy let me know that this was about to be one hell of a night if she was going do at least half the shit she was doing at visitation.

***

"What's on your mind?" Chloe asked as we sat on the plane waiting for takeoff.

"A whole lot and then nothing at all." I answered. Last night was everything she promised. A nigga nut so much I was sure my dick was broken. Her ass had me eating Lobster and shrimp while she was riding my dick. Then she turned her pussy into a sundae and I ate that shit too.

"I want to reach out to Dynastii." I blurted out.

"What? Y'all don't have anything to talk about. Fuck you mean you want to reach out to her?" she snapped.

"Bitch, I know you going watch who the fuck you talking

to!" I said shooting her ass a look to let her know she bet not say anything.

"Ya know what, fine. I'm going take a nap." She said standing up and walking to the back. At the end of the day, it was something about Dynastii I couldn't let go. Nothing seemed right if it didn't involve her. I felt like all I needed to do was explain the situation and we could work this shit out. Unfortunately, I would never get that chance.

Chapter 24:

Tec

"Aww hell naw. Nigga you still in the bed?" Sage asked walking in my house like he owned the bitch. Sitting at the edge of the bed, he started flipping through mail.

"I'm sick. Why you in my house Sage? Is that my fucking mail?" I replied flipping the channels.

"You sick huh? What's wrong then?" He asked like he didn't believe a nigga.

"I think I might have the flu." I lied adding a fake ass cough.

"I'm about to call aunt B and let her know Dynastii got you in here crying like a lil bitch! Talking about you got the flu. You ain't got no motherfucking flu with that dry ass Eazy E cough you just tried to slide in there. You know where she at, go get her ass!" He said making me shake my head no. I knew exactly where Dynastii was but I didn't know how to approach the situation yet. On top of that, I wanted to give her time with her son. Shit was crazy how everything played out but I was glad she got him in the end. Come to find out the lil boy I was bonding with, was hers the whole damn time.

"Aye, I can have these coupons?" He asked holding up some Church's coupons.

"Going through people mail is a crime." I said waving him off. He wasn't even paying attention to me because he had opened one of my letters. I ignored his ass because I rarely went through my own mail.

"Say, Mir you might want to read this." He said throwing

the letter my way. I let it fall to the bed until his next words. "It's from Dynastii."

***

"Why we can't just go out there and snatch their asses up?" Mizanii ghetto ass asked getting tired of sitting in the room. I don't know why I allowed her ass to come but I was regretting it. It was supposed to only be safe and I but for some reason their ass was suddenly joined at the hip. Always in each other face and shit. I already know that if Dynastii was fucking with me, I wouldn't be bothered. I was straight up hating. My mind drifted off to her and a nigga felt like he couldn't breathe. I loved the fuck out of Dynastii and wanted nothing but for her to be happy. With me! All the stressing she was doing, I was about to end that shit. I had my people look into that information she slid me and decided to handle the rest from there when it was confirmed. We were currently in the bedroom of a private plane about to end two big ass stress factors for her.

"Listen." I said as I heard the sound of heels walking to the back where we were. Mizanii ass was too happy for action and she stood to her feet while grabbing her gun.

"You better not fucking shoot that in here!" Sage told her looking scared as hell. He hated flying and that shit was comical to me.

"Why not?" She asked like she wanted to cry that she couldn't shoot someone.

"Cause that shit may make the plane fall out the fucking sky!" He said.

"So, what I'm supposed to do?" Mizanii asked rolling her eyes.

"Ma, you can pinch the bitch to death if you want to. Just don't shoot that shit!" He said doing a sign of the cross. Just as he finished the door opened and this bad ass white bitch walked in. I knew who Chloe was from her hanging with Ashanti but I also knew her ass was crazy. Before she was all the way in the room, Mizanii had wrapped her hand around her mouth and dragged her in.

"Scream and I promise that'll be the last noise you ever make! Understood?" Mizanii asked and Chloe simply nodded with tears falling down her face. "Good." She said before releasing her.

"Where is Prez?" I calmly asked.

"Sitting out front. He said he was thinking." She quickly said.

"What do you have to do with my brother's murder?" I asked. After finding out my brother was on some snake shit, I wasn't as hurt as I should have been.

"N-Nothing. That was all Ashanti's doing." She answered making sure she kept Prez out of it. "Ashanti planned it and actually pulled the trigger to make it look accidental. I only know because she told me." Her ass was snitching without any persuasion needed.

"Where is Ashanti?" I asked.

"I wish I knew. I owe that bitch one!" She spat. Nodding at Mizanii, I gave her the green light to end Chloe's life. Her ass was no more use to me. with a smile Mizanii grabbed her by the hair and quickly slit her throat. That shit was like a movie how the blood slowly oozed out before it just began gushing. Mizanii kept cutting until her neck was barely hanging on, then she finally dropped her body. Walking out of the bedroom, I was tired of hiding. I walked up behind Prez before slapping him behind the head. When he spun around, I watched fear fill his eyes. That shit only pissed me off more. What type of pussy nigga was he?

"T-Tec?" He asked.

"In the flesh, but you knew that." I replied taking a seat next to him. "I think it's time we had a talk, man to pussy." I said. "I call you a pussy for multiple reasons but the biggest one being that your ass was just goin leave the country. You didn't even care to check on your seed. Where the fuck they make you type of niggas at?" I spat.

"I didn't want a child. Both of them bitches knew that!" He said. Before I could say anything Mizanii had walked in and brought her glock down across his head.

"Watch your fucking mouth when you speak on Dynastii." She calmly replied as she and Sage sat in the other chair available. Prez shit was leaking but he was trying hard not to show weakness. He failed.

"I'm leaving the country, you don't have to worry about me bruh." He pleaded.

"Oh, I'm not worried but you leaving the country ain't enough. I don't want your ass on the same fucking planet as my girl. I don't want her stressing no more and you were a big stress factor. Why Ahmad? Why did y'all go after him?" I asked.

"Man, that was all Ashanti's idea. Her ass wanted the stash he had and she thought you would take over. I hit his stash first though. It was strictly about the money and drugs for me, I didn't kill your brother though." He confessed.

"But you tried." I said knowing now that he got the charge for shooting Ahmad's right-hand man. When he didn't answer my question, that let me know he was guilty. I watched as Sage walked up behind him and waited for my cue. "One more question, how you feel about me raising you son. Once we get rid of y'all bodies, I'm going get my family. Malakhi needs to know what a real man is, and I plan to show him." I said smiling at the thought. I was already on a plane, why not go get my woman. I didn't wait on a response as I nodded at Sage. The sound of him snapping Prez's neck did nothing for me. My brother was still a snake, before death. And I didn't know how to fix Dynastii and I.

I knew that I wasn't willing to let her walk away and I was willing to make myself look like a fool to prove it.

Chapter 25:

Ashanti

"Chloe, what the fuck? I've been calling you for days, I really need some help. I have to leave the country. I don't know how but someone knows something, please call me." My voice broke as I ended the hundredth voicemail I had left on her cell phone. Chloe never left me hanging like she's doing now. If you ask me she has no reason to. I mean she has a reason to but she doesn't know that. According to what she knows, I've been an amazing friend to her. Now according to what I know, she had every right to leave me high and dry. I had violated in the worse way. I fucked around and ruined her family and the sad part was if I could go back to the day it started, I wouldn't change shit.

"Where are you going?" Chloe asked stirring from her sleep.

"To the restroom and get me something to drink, go back to sleep." I replied crossing over her. I stood in the room for a second and listened as she fell back asleep and her snores filled the room before I slid out of the pajama pants and top I was wearing. At the tender age of 16 I was stacked. I had my boyfriend at the time to thank for that. Fucking was our favorite form of exercise and thanks to him, my ass was full grown and so were my breast and my hips. The problem was, he no longer satisfied me. He was too broke to spoil me like Chloe was spoiled and his dick wasn't big enough for what I was looking for. Plus, my sights were on someone else, someone who could spoil me like Chloe was spoiled and fuck me like a grown man. I knew because he was a grown man and he was the very person who spoiled her. I was tired of getting gifts because she had to beg him to buy me something. I wanted gifts because he wanted to gift them to me. On top of that, I saw the way he looked at me when I was around the house. He

was too scared to make the move so I made mine first.

Walking into Chloe's bathroom that was connected to her room, I took a hoe bath. Making sure all my hot spots were smelling fresh, I even did a spot shave. My boyfriend thought eating pussy was nasty but from the first time I saw it being done on Playboy channel, I knew I wanted my pussy in someone's mouth. That someone would have to be, Lance. Yep, my best friend's dad. After coming my wrap down, I smiled at my reflection. I had my plan all figured out. Her mom was on a trip for the weekend and I knew her father would be pouring in late. As soon as I heard him arrive, I started dripping wet. I knew he would play with his drugs and pass out so I lay in the dark and did a countdown until I made my move.

Tip toeing into her bedroom, I dug in her draw for the lace bra and panty set I knew was in here. When we went to the mall earlier today, I swapped out a pair of her millions of bra and panties sets and got my size in a few. She selfishly didn't even offer me. I got Mr. Lance's favorite color, red and slid them on. I quietly applied lotion to my entire body so that my skin was baby smooth and glistened. Stealing her mac lip glass, I lathered my lips then slid out of the room closing the door behind me. The trip down the stairs was quiet except for the sound of the television playing. Leaving the lights off, I paused in the living room where I took in what I knew her mom couldn't possibly handle. That lil ass white woman couldn't take all the dick that was hanging out of his boxers. I licked my lips before deciding that it was time for him to wake up. I saw the remnants of the drugs on the table and didn't give a damn as long as his dick still worked. I turned off the television so that it was pitch black and walked back towards the hallway. Thank God for my drama classes, I was about to perform. Knocking down a book I heard him began to move and started the fake crying as I ran to the living room and sat my ass right on his dick.

"What the fuck?" He called out in the dark.

"Mr. Lance, is that you?" I questioned like it was a surprise he was sitting there. Thing is, I never made a move to get off of his lap.

Instead, I slightly grinded my ass until I felt a reaction from his dick. Finally, I popped up and leaned forward to turn on the lap that sat in the corner of where he was sitting. When the light came on his eyes traveled up the length of my body and fell on my ass. His dick woke up before he fully did.

"Where are your clothes?" He asked trying to hide his massive dick and attempting to focus on my face. At this point I was upright with my perky C cups in his face.

"I'm so sorry. I thought Chloe and I were still alone. I was on the phone with my boyfriend... well ex-boyfriend and he- he broke up with me." I lied my ass off and fell back into a fit of tears. Before he could react, I was back in his lap and crying on his shoulder. "I don't understand." I cried out.

"I'm sure it will work itself out Ashanti but you have to go put some clothes on." He damn near moaned out as I wiggled on his lap. His dick was poking against my pussy with the thin lace being the only thing separating us and I was sure he felt how wet I was.

"I'm not sure if it'll work out this time. I just want to kill myself." I dramatically replied.

"Why would you say something like that? Any man would be happy to have you. I don't know why he broke up with you but it is definetly his loss." He snapped back in father mode. "Tell me what happened?" He said exactly what I wanted him to say. The drugs were slowly putting him back to sleep and I was happy for that. Sitting on his lap, I talked and talked for over an hour until he was back snoring. Climbing off his lap, I turned the light back off and removed my bra and panties. Falling to my knees, I gripped his dick firmly before licking and kissing along it. The subtle moans from his drug induced sleep was all the motivation for me to take his dick into my mouth. I gave head before and could normally fit all of James' dick in my mouth but that wasn't the case with Mr. Lance, it was too damn big. Although my jaw was hurting, I kept sucking his dick until it was hard and I was nice and wet. Standing onto the couch, I straddled him then eased my pussy down on his dick. The pain was no joke but I was determined to get to the pleasure.

"Oooohhhh shit." I moaned out as I slide further down until my pussy lips were spread as far as they would go. I sat for a second and rotated my hips so that I could adjust to his size but the feeling must have woken him from his sleep.

"God damn!" He whispered as I gently glided. "I thought you only like missionary?" He asked letting me know he thought I was Chloe's mom. I was good with that as long as he didn't take his dick out of my pussy. With my feet planted firmly onto either side of his thighs, I began to bounce and grind on his dick. The pain was gone and it was just pleasure as he thrust up every time I came down.

"Fuck me!" I accidently said and felt him tense up. When I felt his arm reach out, I was sure he was about to turn on the light so I began bouncing faster.

"Awww shit!" he called out flipping on the light. "Ashanti! What are you doing?" He called out loudly, causing me to cover his mouth.

"Shhh, you don't want Chloe to see you fucking her friend!" I said still riding his dick. I was being cheated out of life fucking James, this was how I was supposed to be fucked.

"You. Are. A Child!" He said in a harsh whisper as his eyes rolled to the back of his head.

"And I'm fucking you better than your wife!" I spat back rotating around with his dick still inside of me. I had watched him look at my ass too often and knew he would enjoy seeing it bounce on his dick. When I felt his hands grip my hips, I knew he wouldn't make me get off of him. The only sounds heard were our muffled moans and the sounds my pussy was making. Leaning back, I grabbed his neck and pulled him closer. "I know you're tired of fucking a blow up doll." I moaned out taking a jab at Chloe's mom. Instead of answering, he flipped me over so that I was leaning over the couch and punished my pussy. It wasn't long before we were both coming and he pulled out of me. When he walked away, I thought that was the end of my fantasy play so I slid my panties and bra on before heading back up the stairs. Mr. Lance had other plans, before I could open Chloe's door, he wrapped his hand around my mouth and dragged me to the room he shared with his wife.

"You better not tell anyone shit about this!" he said ripping the thong off of my body. Pushing me back on the bed, he dived head first into my pussy with his mouth. "This is my pussy, you hear me? No one better even sniff what's mine!" He spoke with a mouth full of my wet pussy." The feeling was indescribable and I knew I was hooked but even at sixteen I knew to keep my mind on my money.

"I won't tell about this or share your pussy as long as you keep me happy!" I replied grinding my pussy in his face. When he looked up with my juices dripping from his mouth I knew he would need a little more convincing. That night I became his person freak while my best friend slept in the next room. He fucked me in every hole but my ear and when I crawled out of there in the morning, I had a debit card and cash. For six months, we fucked daily whether it was in his house or at a hotel. He was in love and I was paid, fair exchange. It was all good until I got pregnant. I didn't know he would leave his wife nor did I know that he would get me my own spot. It was fine until he started smothering me so I invited his daughter to move in with me in hopes that he would stay away. That shit only made him start sneaking in at night. Our relationship ended when he found out I aborted his child. Fuck what he thought, I wasn't trying to be a mother. I was fine though, because soon after I met Tec, then Ahmad, then Prez. I was set. Or so I thought.

The ringing of my phone pulled my attention away from my memories and into my current fucked up ass situation. My greed had got the best of me and my secrets were spilling out without my permission. I had been getting threatening text messages from Tec and Dynastii and knew it would not be long before they caught up to me. Desperate times called for desperate measures and I didn't even have to come up with a plan, one fell in my lap. Something that I rarely done was stray from the little one-bedroom home I was renting but yesterday I had to and I was the luckiest woman alive. I had no idea how they found me but as I was grocery shopping, two female detectives pulled me to the side. According to them, they had been tipped off about some murders that Tec and a female accomplice had done together and needed my help to lock them away forever. I was offered protection, housing and money which was music to my ears since my account was nonexistent. I didn't know what female accomplice they had in mind but I was giving them Dynastii then starting a new life. Like clockwork, there was a knock at the door causing me to jump. Checking the window, I was able to breathe easy knowing I was about to be put into protective custody.

"Good morning, did you do like we asked?" Asked the bright skinned detective. I don't know how to gorgeous women ended up in this field of work but it could never be me.

"Good morning, yes I did. I left the note saying I went away because I needed to be alone and I would call when I got there. I left everything as is except that one bag and I'll leave my cell phone here. You will buy me another one, right Detective…" I trailed off because I couldn't remember her name.

"Sinaya, just call me Sinaya. And this is my partner Blessing." She replied with a smile. Something about her was warm and inviting. "And the government will provide you with everything you will need for the afterlife." She said making me look at her weird.

"The afterlife?" I questioned.

"That's what Blessing and I call it when we do what we do." She assured me. "Let's get out of here. We have to make a stop and get your paperwork in order." She said.

"Wait, I thought you would do that before coming to get me. And how are we going wherever we going? Wait, where are we going? I don't even know where you are taking me." I blabbed getting nervous. Tec's reach was far and I didn't want to be on the receiving end of his anger. I didn't even notice that Sinaya had started pacing off to the corner. "What's wrong with her?" I asked the other detective.

"She does that often. Your questions will be answered once we are in the safety of the car. There is no telling who already knows where you are." She replied.

"They won't find me." I answered.

"We did." She said making sense. Without a second thought, I grabbed my bag and left everything else behind. Following them to the car, I slid in and within seconds we were on the road. Quietness filled the car for a moment before Sinaya spoke.

"So, who is Tec's female accomplice?" She asked getting straight to the point.

"Dynastii. I don't know her last name but she was dating Tec. She has a son and her ex is in police custody, President Pierre. He is the father of her child." I snitched as a thought crossed my mind. I didn't need Prez coming after me for his money either. "President actually has something to do with this also." I quickly added.

"And how do you know President?" Blessing asked.

"Am, I safe. Like if I reveal my involvement will you give me like some type of immunity?" I asked. Watching Law and Order and Criminal Minds was paying off. I wasn't so green to this shit.

"Yeah, we will offer you immunity." Blessing said with a look on her face I couldn't read.

"Well, Prez and I were messing around while I was dating Tec. I was also messing with Tec's brother Ahmad. Ahmad was heavy in the streets and together Prez and I came up with a plan to make us both well off. We were supposed to kill Ahmad but when it was time to do it, I changed my mind. Prez didn't. He killed Ahmad and that's why he is in jail, the only reason Tec doesn't know is because his auntie is keeping it away from him."

I replied telling half the truth. Prez didn't come up with the plan at all, I did. His dumb ass killed the wrong person though and I had to get rid of Ahmad when it was all said and done. My plan was to snatch up his stash and then force Tec back into the streets where he and I could get the fame his brother had. You see Ahmad and I were fucking on the low for a while but his ass wasn't as loose with his funds as his brother. When he decided he wouldn't treat me like I was accustomed to being treated, my plan was put into action.

"You went to visit Prez, why? What ties do you two have to each other?" Blessing asked. The purpose for those visits was to force him to bond with his son. But I wasn't about to expose my biggest secret. I just couldn't.

"To discuss money." I easily lied. "Can we talk later, I'm a little tired." I lied again. I needed to think and choose my lies wisely so that nothing came back to me. For what felt like forever we drove until we finally pulled up to a nice sized older home. "What is this?" I asked.

"The beginning to you crossing over to the afterlife." Sinaya answered stepping out of the car with Blessing right behind her. Something told me I should be scared but they were detectives. I had to be safe, right? I followed them into the house and surprisingly we weren't alone. There were a group of people already sitting there. "What's going on Sinaya and Blessing?" I asked them confused as hell.

"Nah ma, you can call me Sin and that's Beretta. It's like we said, you are crossing over to the afterlife today." Sinaya said dropping her proper tone. A woman with wild curly purple hair came from another room of the house.

"Hey, I'm Purp. I heard you like snatching children and shit huh?" She said causing my eyes to damn near pop from my head. Who the fuck were these people? "I see you look a lil shocked you'll get answers when you wake up." She said before her fist slammed into my face repeatedly until I blacked out

174

from the pain.

Chapter 26:

Dynastii

I had never been so excited to catch a body in my entire life. I would forever owe Sunjai and her family for helping me out with the many pieces to this one puzzle. When I first met Sunjai, she was a fraction of the woman she is today. She had let a man break her and was running from a life she claimed she didn't want anymore. It's funny that we escaped to the same island for different reasons. I was there to learn my son all over again and to keep him safe. She was there because she needed to know herself again. After a few conversations, she knew what she needed to do but I was just as lost as ever. It was her time to offer me help in the form of her crazy ass family. I got the answers I needed and then they helped me to pull off the best revenge ever. The satisfaction I felt fill my body when her fear left her body in the form of that scream and the piss that puddled around the chair she sat in from the sight of me.

"Dy-Dynastii, I'm so sorry!" She said before crying her heart out. "I'm so sorry, I never meant for things to end up like this."

"No bitch you never meant to get caught! I have a couple of questions, before you die go ahead and answer that." I said holding a rusty machete. Once she heard me say she was going to die she began crying even harder.

"Oh, this bitch cry way too much. Was your ass crying when you were acting like her baby's mama with your sick ass. Can I beat her?" Sunjai asked causing me to laugh. I had to admit having her and her crew her made shit easy and a lot more fun.

Their asses kept the jokes coming and it was just what I needed to calm down.

"Why my son?" I asked her the most important question. The fact that this was the quietest the house had been since we got here let me know that we all wanted to know the same answer.

"It wasn't my idea, I swear. You have to understand, mother to mother, losing a child is already hard. Then you have my situation which is worse. He was... He was alive and well when we went to sleep. I checked on him like... like at least five times, Dynastii he was fine." She paused and let out a cry that had nothing to do with her fear of being in a room full of killers knowing her life was the next for the taken. "I was soooo tired and I just wanted him near so I could stop walking over to his room. We fell asleep together, him on side of me. Four hours, that's how long it took for me to realize my baby hadn't woke up. I only knew something was wrong because Prez showed up to my house. It wasn't normally for him to pop up whenever y'all would fight. My baby was so cold when I touched him. So cold and stiff and I knew, that something was wrong. He had no pulse and wasn't breathing." She told her story and for a second my heart went out to her. I wasn't some monster with no compassion.

"I'm really sorry this happened to you but I'm having on hell of a time understanding why Malakhi got pulled into this." I said forcing not a single tear to fall from my eye.

"It wasn't my idea. My Ezra was Malachi's brother. Despite him not wanting anything to do with either of our kids, Prez didn't care about me having Ezra. You having Malakhi, however, he hated that shit. He complained about it all the time. How having a baby made you soft and it made you change for the worse. So, he told me not to call the ambulance and he would make it all alright. He said I had probably suffocated my own baby and I would end up in jail. I believed him when he said he would make it alright and that I could have another baby. Days later, he brought me Malakhi. They were twins and I refused to question why I could all of a sudden have him. All I know is my son's body was gone and another was presented to me." When she slightly smiled I fucking lost it.

"You. Don't. Just. Take. Someone's. Child. As. Your. Own!" I said and in between each word delivering a blow to her face. "For MONTHS, they ran my story on the news." I paused to will, myself to stop crying. "Bitch you killed your child, not me! Why did I have to suffer?" I felt a hand on my shoulder and turned to see Sin calling me off to the side. We walked out and I heard Beretta, Sunjai and Purp fucking Ashanti up.

"Don't kill her!" Sin screamed out. I don't know why, I got all the questions I needed.

"What's up?" I asked slowly catching my breath.

"You needed a break. Don't forget you have a bun in the oven ma." She reminded me.

"I don't even want this baby. I don't want anything to do with Tec." I told her what I had been going back and forth trying to decide. In my heart I felt like I was done with Amir.

"You ready to leave the only man that really had you? For what?" She asked and I was already aggravated with that question before she finished it. I told them our history and how I found him in that bed already. So why was she acting like I was tripping?

"He was in that bitch's bed!" I damn near shouted.

"Bitch and! You said it yourself that his ass seemed out of it. You never know what the fuck happened! I'm going tell you this because I was you once upon a time. The difference was, my nigga cheated and had a whole fucking baby on the way. May it Rest In Peace. The ways she said that sent chills down my arm. This bitch was crazier than me so I know she had something to do with that child's death. "Make that nigga know what it's like to miss you! Make that nigga as sick as he made you! Then move on with your man if he's as good of a man as you thought he was prior to that situation! You shot out on his ass for months without knowing facts." She said before walking out and snatching her gun from the small of her back. I quickly followed out of curiosity.

"What the hell are you doing?" I asked.

"Getting answers. Y'all back up." She told the girls who were stomping Ashanti ass out. When I saw her face, I didn't even recognize her. She wasn't unconscious though, she was crying in the fetal position. Sin clicked the safety off and pointed the gun at her head. "Lie to me and I'm sending you meet your fucking child. Why was Tec in your bed?" She asked.

"I called him over. I wanted to fuck but he refused. I even drugged him but he managed to fight me off. Nothing happened, we just fell asleep. l she said coughing out blood. I was a little excited about that information for some reason. Suddenly, a thought popped into my head.

"Did... Did Tec know you had my baby?" I needed her answer to be no. If she told me anything else, I would have to kill Tec.

"Only Prez, myself and Chloe knew." She confirmed. Grabbing Sin's gun, I emptied the clip into her forehead. My intentions were to torture her like Sin and Beretta told me but life tortured her enough. After hearing her child's death, I just wanted to head back to Turks and Caicos and love on my baby.

***

Walking into the beach house, I handed Reign the things she asked for from the store.

"Did y'all have fun?" She asked looking said. I shook my head at all the women in this family. Only their asses would think this was fun.

"Don't even answer her ass. She had a lot of fun right here

with me." Her husband Rello answered walking up and rubbing her swollen belly. I didn't know how she was going do it dealing with his ass. Something was wrong with him. They were having a boy and he was mad that would not name the child, Junior Junior. I thought it was a joke until I found out their daughter's name was changed from Royalty to Rello Jr. The fuck kind of shit is that?

"Where is my baby?" I asked ignoring those two. Rello gave me a damn headache when we spoke but I got good vibes from them all. That was the only reason I was able to leave and handle Ashanti's ass. I trusted Reign and Ghost with my son. I didn't trust Streets or Rello to have my child acting like their asses when I got back.

"He outside bonding." Rello said with a sneaky grin.

"Bounding with who?" I asked Praying it wasn't Streets.

"Shit, I don't know. The men!" He replied pulling Reign away to a room. All their asses did was fuck and that's why they're in the situation they're in now. She was excited for her pregnancy and he was even more excited than her. She told me how many doctors appointments and trials they went through until they were finally successful in getting pregnant. Grabbing the things I brought for Malakhi, I went outside in search of him. What I didn't expect was to walk out to him playing in the sand with my sister. I dropped everything at the door and ran over to both of them fully aware that all eyes were on us.

"Mizanii!" I called out while hugging her like it had been years. Z and I were always close so the time away from each other was hard. "How did you get here?" I asked.

"Shit if I knew you were living like this, I would have been here a long time ago. Where were you, we have been here for days." She asked.

"Taking care of Ashanti." I replied.

"Well Prez and Chloe were taken care of too." She surprised me.

"How?" I asked. Instead of answering she motioned behind me where I turned around and immediately the tears fell from my eyes. Tec was down on one knee with Malakhi right next to him on one knee also. My baby looked so handsome in his all white like Tec's.

"I had to get lil man to get on one knee with me because I knew you wouldn't turn me down if he was giving me permission to marry his mom. Right lil man?" He asked Malakhi.

"Right! Will you marry me?" Malakhi said like it was rehearsed.

"Woah woah woah! How you steal my line? Remember I got some things to say then I say that and you say the other line." Tec said laughing.

"Oh yeah, then hurry up!" Malachi said causing everyone to laugh.

"I got this bruh." He said before looking back at me. "I was wrong, but not in the way you think I was wrong. I would never purposely disrespect you! There ain't a woman alive that makes me as happy as you do and I would be stupid to let you walk away from what we have and what we are building. I made myself a promise that I would make sure you never had another moment of sadness and I plan on holding up my word..."

"You finished yet? I'm hungry!" Malachi interrupted causing us to laugh.

"Aye, give me my money back!" He said side eyeing my baby.

"I was just playing!" Malachi answered quickly.

"Look, let me wrap it up since we have a lil blocker. I'm ready for us three to be a family. I want to give you and Malachi both what y'all deserve. Ma give me a second chance; will you marry me?" He finished before looking at Malachi like he was crazy. "You killing me!" He laughed when Malachi didn't say anything.

"Oh, my bad. Mama please don't say no!" He said happy that he remembered his line.

"I have to say no baby." I said to Malakhi as I watched the smile fall from Tec's face. He said three of us and its four of us. He's leaving someone out!" I said rubbing my stomach. Shock crossed his face before he jumped up and grabbed me.

"Stop fucking lying!" He said as he laughed. Grabbing my hand, he slipped the ring on my finger.

"I didn't say yeah!" I reminded him.

"You didn't have a choice after telling me that! This is my family!" He said lifting me from my feet and placing a kiss on my lips. I heard everyone clapping but I felt him walking away from everyone and we had the same though on our mind as I wrapped my thing legs around his waist. I couldn't help that I loved him. And I didn't want too, Shawty fell for a boss.

The End

Sneak Peek:

Rise of The New Mafia Dolls

Written By:

Trenae &
Nikki Brown

Not your average doll...

Sza

The tapping of my red and gold pointy toe Jimmy Choo heel calmed my nerves as I ran my hand up and down Zoe's back. I could tell he was trying to hold back the tears in his eyes but was slowly failing that task. I had already witnessed a few trailing down his cheeks. As fast as they fell, he would catch it then subtly look my way. If he was worried about me judging him, I wouldn't. I had not too long ago been in his very shoes. I remember sitting in the front pew of my mother's funeral surrounded by people who were only there to see how lavish the funeral would be and if she left them any money. I couldn't help but to shake my head as I looked at Zoe's auntie putting on a performance that would rival Tamar Braxton from the BET awards. Lil baby didn't even like Zoe's mother so I definitely had to stifle a laugh.

"You good?" Zoe whispered thinking I was chocking and I went with it.

"Yeah, I'm just going to step out and get me some water. Did y'all still want Kaliyah, Jayde and I to read the eulogy?" I inquired in my own whisper.

"If you think you can, anyone else would be too extra and fake. In the short time she had met you, my mom loved you like a daughter." He said causing me to smile despite the circumstances.

"I'm glad we were able to bond before her passing. Let me go get that sip of water." I said standing to my feet. I was small in stature but my presence was giant. My father made sure that I knew from birth that, even a midget could command a room with no problem. Stepping into the waiting area of the funeral home, I bumped into Zoe's father. Big Zoe hated me with a passion and never hid his dislike for me. I never did him anything, he said he just had a bad vibe from me. I wasn't in the business of persuading anyone to be fond of me so, that was on him.

"How disrespectful to wear red at my wife's funeral." He spat eyeing my shoes and matching blazer.

"I'm sorry you see it as a sign of disrespect, sir. Zoe actually got me these to match his attire. After all, your wife's favorite color was red. And disrespect, is having you mistress and illegitimate child, present at your wife's funeral like you were all one big happy family. If she were already buried, Mrs. Hillaire would be rolling in her grave by now." I smiled as his eyes bulged at the fact that I knew his well-kept secret. "I'll leave you to think about that." I said patting his shoulder and heading to the lady's room. After checking my makeup and making sure that it was just right, I applied a little lip gloss and walked out into a now empty hallway. Peeping into the funeral home I noticed everyone including, Mr. Hillaire were inside. It was easy to locate him because the funeral home though huge, was empty. Zoe requested just the family be in attendance and since his family was small, this was it. The song that Kaliyah was singing had finally come to an end so I walked back in and up to the podium, as the doors closed behind me. Standing next to the casket I was able to take a better look at her body and you couldn't tell that she died from a single gunshot to the head.

"Thank you all for joining the Hillaire family as they pay the final respects and say their farewells to Lace Hillaire." I said before Jayde took over.

"Who was Lace Hillaire?" She asked reading from the note card she wrote out. "Lace Hillaire was the epitome of Southern Class. She had grace, style and that old fashion southern charm that we all grew accustomed to. Not one single person could be in her presence and not feel welcomed." She finished.

"When I first met, Lace Hillaire, she greeted me as if we were old friends instead of me being the woman after her son's heart." Kaliyah spoke smiling in Kyle's direction. "There is no other way to put it except, Lace Hillaire's time here was cut short too soon. There was still so much for her to accomplish and so many more people for her to touch in her own special way." She finished as I took over.

"Lace Hillaire leaves behind to mourn her death, her husband, Alonzo Hillaire. She also leaves behind, their three sons, Alonzo Jr., Kyle and Joshua Hillaire. And unbeknownst to her, she leaves behind a step son, Lonzo. Who is seated in the back with his mother, Elise, please stand?" I requested as everyone but Alonzo Sr. turned to the back and gasped at the resemblance between them and his brothers. I noticed Jayde easing her hand into the casket and smirked. I had to thank Zoe for making sure no one was able to bring weapons in. Everyone was checked, except Lace Hillaire of course.

"HOW DARE YOU MAKE A MOCKERY OF MY WIFE'S FUNERAL?" He roared.

"Nigga, how dare you make a mockery of your wife, the fuck?" Jayde asked causing me to hit her. "The fuck you hit me for?" she asked.

"We in a funeral home and you cursing." I said.

"We about to do way worse than cursing and that's what you worried about?" she asked as Zoe and his brothers turned back to us.

"Z, what is all this? You had to do this shit here?" He asked all in his feelings. I immediately rolled my eyes at his soft ass.

"Always business baby, never personal." I replied reaching in the casket and grabbing my favorite twins, Bonnie and Clyde. My gold desert eagles were a gift from my mom on my 16th birthday and I had never missed a target with these pretty motherfuckers. "Listen up because I don't like repeating myself." I said noticing Jayde and Kaliyah had grabbed their weapons too.

"I knew there was something about those bitches!" Alonzo Sr. spat.

"Yeah well, you should have gone with your first mind, pimp. Instead, you was listening to your tender dick sons and ole Lace here." Jayde replied patting the dead woman on the forehead and making me shake my head. Jayde was as hood as they came and didn't try to hide it. At that exact moment Alonzo Sr, attempted to run at us and was instantly stopped when two bullets from Kaliyah's berettas entered each of his thighs.

"Let's not have any more uncalled-for ass accidents until I say my peace okay?" I said rolling my eyes. "Now, we are known as the New Mafia Dolls. You may not have heard of us, but you damn sure heard of New Mafia. New Mafia will never take disrespect and when you decided to move product in their states without paying your due, that was disrespectful. Now our pops are fair, so they did reach out to you and offer a partnership. Your father, declined. In fact, he called my father a pussy ass nigga before declining. And, he disrespected me one time too many." I said before a single bullet pierced his forehead. He didn't see or hear it coming because of the silencer. I looked into Zoe's shocked eyes before sending a bullet through his head also. Within seconds, everyone in the funeral home met the same demise. No words had to be said as we walked out the doors and slide into the awaiting blacked out Hummer.

"Everything good?" Tony asked from the driver seat.

"Better than good." We all answered as flames engulfed the funeral home and we pulled off.

I let out a sigh of relief because we had successfully completed this mission after three long ass months. Our fathers were skeptical about our roles in the New Mafia, but we quickly put those worries to rest. Just this morning every dime the Hillaire family owned was split into our accounts and the whole family business was put to rest all because of the New Mafia Dolls. What is a New Mafia Doll you ask? A New Mafia Doll is a fucking terror released on you by the New Mafia organization.

You only see a New Mafia Doll when she wants to be seen and that's an omen worst that the grim. No one knows of us, but the remains we leave in a burning grave once our job is done and our fathers, the heads of the New Mafia.

Our job is simple, end any threat that comes our way. Could our father's handle their own drama? Sure, they could go in and kill everything breathing. The problem is, most threats will take their valuable information to the grave. It takes a special kind of woman to get the grimiest of savages to pillow talk, and that's where we come in. We have never walked away empty handed and we always get out mark. In a man's world, sometimes you have to send a doll to get shit done.

Chapter 1:

Sza

*I be in and out them banks so much
I know they're tired of me.*

Honestly, don't give a fuck 'bout who ain't fond of me!

*Dropped two mixtapes in six months,
what bitch working as hard as me?*

I had Cardi B's Bodak Yellow blasting through my beats as I hit my 6th mile on the treadmill. In high school when I wasn't training, I was running track and now running was my stress reliever. It had only been two months since our last mission and the New Mafia already had us on our next one without anytime to breath. Apparently, the St. Julien's decided they didn't want a partnership with the New Mafia, but they wanted their territories. What was crazy was the fact that they had a sit down with the heads of the New Mafia like they understood everything only to change their minds. Well, in the eyes of my father, that was disrespect. So here we were, making sure everyone got the message that disrespect would not be taken lightly. I looked up just in time to see Jayde waving her arms and rolled my eyes. I already knew she was about to complain about the lengthy work out. Hitting pause on my treadmill, I removed the headphones and looked her way.

"Yo, Flo Jo!" She called out always the joker of the crew. "Ma, I know this running shit seems fun to you and I respect that. On God, I can think about a million more things I would rather do than take another step on that machine." She said as

Kaliyah stood to her left side agreeing.

I looked at their attire and knew that their asses weren't into this anyway. I lowkey think they only came because they wanted to wear the slutty ass workout wear. Jayde's ass was damn near hanging out of the white and black Pink track suit. The top was a cropped hoodie and the bottoms were damn near panties. If she had just a little more ass, they would be thongs. That was the crazy thing about Jayde, she wasn't into the girly shit that most girls were into, but she loved the fuck out of showing off her petite shape.

While Kaliyah and I would go crazy over some red bottoms her ass was going crazy of the next Jordan release. Kaliyah was wearing the fuck out of a Pink all in one jumpsuit. I know it was made for active wear however, it had thot written all over it. Kaliyah had the physique and beauty of a run way model so it didn't look as thotty on her until you got to the top half. There were no zippers, buttons or anything holding it together. It literally was held in place by her perky breast.

"They look nice huh?" Kaliyah blew a kiss my way catching me eyeing her breast.

"You know I'm jealous as fuck. They look like you got them done when I'm knowing you were just blessed." I joked stepping off the treadmill and wiping my face with the towel that hung on the arm of the machine. "My bad, I was in my zone and had even forgot y'all were here." I confessed as we walked out of the in-home gym.

We were housed in a mini mansion right off the beach. Normally, we would be in something more modest but according to my father, we would be on this mission for a while. He felt that this crime family would be harder to penetrate. I thought otherwise. Our fathers always wanted to see us as their little princess and they had us fucked up. Yes, we called ourselves dolls, but we could and did outshoot the big boys. We were that silent threat that snuck on up on you and by time you realized what was going on, it was too late. By the first greeting, we were already spreading through your organization like a bad virus on a computer.

"We already know, you always get like this before we began a new mission." Jayde observed.

"Like what?" I asked.

"First, your ass works out like Robocop in this bitch. Like, no breaks or anything Then, you get really distant from us. You lock yourself up in your room and just study your mission. Yo ass didn't even study that damn hard for the S.A.T's It's like an obsession, if you ask me." She finished with a shrug.

"Good thing I'm not asking you, huh?" I replied. "You don't get it, I know that your fathers are head of the New Mafia's also, but I get it harder than you do. At least y'all have mother's that shield you two from the wrath of our father's, I don't have that. Look at Kamiyah, she up and left the dolls with no looking back. I admire the fact that she stood up to our fathers and now she has a life of her own. I don't say anything because I know you miss your sister Kaliyah, but I keep up with her. She is doing the damn thing. She seems to be bringing in as much money as we do without all the drama, in fact she seems to be enjoying life. On some for real shit, I wish our last mission lasted longer." I finally let out what was bothering me.

"Why?" Kaliyah questioned. "That's not even like you. You're normally the get in and get out type." She said making me nod my head.

"Yeah, you're right that is my normal mind frame. But being with Zoe made me realize something, I'm lonely. Though I didn't have any feelings for him, I did enjoy being in his presence. The dates, the pillow talk, the gifts, the dick." I said laughing.

"Damn, was he packing?" Jayde asked causing me to quickly nod my head.

"Remember that day you asked me if I hurt my leg?" I asked. "That was all his work."

"What was all his work? When I asked, you said no." she replied.

"Well shit, it wasn't my leg that was hurt. Girl that man had put a hurting on my pussy. I was bowlegged for at least a week. The dick almost saved his life." I said before noticing Kaliyah was in her own world. "What's up with you?" I questioned.

"Shit, you have me thinking. After Kamiyah left, my father pulled me into the dolls and acted as if it should have been an honor. It was easy being that I always trained with the three of you but this wasn't what I wanted. I wanted to model, like mom did. You say our mothers are able to protect us but that's not true. Though they speak up for us, you know who always gets the last word." She said releasing a sigh. "I'm going shower and take a nap before the festivities began." She said walking away.

"How you feel about this?" I asked Jayda who never voiced her emotions. Jayda was the firecracker out of the crew and I think that was because she held so much in. I have never seen her cry or heard her complain about this lifestyle. I think if it wasn't for her fighting, she would have been exploded. We all had our stress relievers. I was a runner and I enjoyed driving fast cars. When I was behind a wheel, no one could fucking touch me. I guess like running did, in my mind I was leaving everything behind. The faster I went, the better I felt. Our lil firecracker Jayde, would much rather be in a boxing ring. We had to keep a close eye on her because she was a loud mouth that backed up every word she spoke, then some. Kaliyah's crazy ass relieved her stress playing with those blades she owns. Her mom taught her all kinds of tricks with knives and blades and she fell in love with that.

"Shit, I don't really have a feeling towards this You see the life we live. We can arrive in any city and shut down their biggest mall. We don't depend on anyone and our bank accounts look like out of country phone numbers. To whom much is given, much is required." She finished with a shrug. Nodding my head, I started to walk away so that I could shower. "Aye, I thought you were about to tell me about the dick?" She called out making me laugh. Ignoring her, I climbed the steps to my portion of the house.

My bedroom could house a medium sized apartment and was decorated to my liking, in all white. I had an infatuation with white and always had since a child. It was rare that you saw me in anything but that color. I quickly stripped down out of the white tights and sports bra I wore and stepped into the shower. The massaging shower head quickly erased any thoughts clouding my mind. The water rained down on me before the smell of my body wash filled the bathroom and I began lathering my body. After thirty minutes of relaxation, I found myself unable to sleep so I reached for the folder that was lying in my bed.

"Knox St. Julien." I read his name aloud and couldn't ignore the fact that my clit jumped as I fingered through the ten photos that were attached with his profile.

I knew everything there was to know about him and even that couldn't prepare me for the meeting that was to take place tonight. Though Jayde thought I was obsessing over him that wasn't the case. I was simply attempting to find an angle. True enough, I had been the reason at least twenty men met their demise after parading me on their arm. That was easy, this wouldn't be. Knox had a fiancée and I had no idea of their bond. She was no threat, honestly, I could simply kill the bitch. The problem, however, would be waiting for his ass to grieve over her. I simply didn't have the time; I would just have to come correct when it came to him. With different ideas running through my head, I attempted to fall asleep again. After all, I would need rest before I ran into Mr. Knox tonight.

COMING SOON!

About The Author

Trenae'

Trenae' is a 28 year old native of Lafayette, La. She was always an avid reader but it wasn't until she read, The Coldest Winter Ever, that Trenae' became infatuated with the urban fiction world. What started as a stress reliever quickly turned into a passion. After stepping out on faith and turning in her manuscript, Trenae' signed her first contract in March 2016. Trenae's debut novel, The Sins Of My Beretta, was released on May 1, 2016. Trenae' is now an independent author.

Made in the USA
Monee, IL
04 September 2020

41251824R00114